HIGH PRAISE FOR THE WRITING OF WAYNE C. LEE

"Lee's commanding grasp of history is combined with a colorful storytelling."
—*Midwest Book Review* on *Bad Men & Bad Towns*

"*Trails of the Smoky Hill* is a rip-roaring account of the Old West."
—*The Neshoba Democrat*

"An excellent example of what can be done with a vast amount of material, and contributes a worthwhile study for the beginning history buff."
—*True West Magazine* on *Deadly Days in Kansas*

D1013541

3 MB

Neighbor vs. Neighbor

Within the hour, Dan Ferry would be on the Triangle F—if he wasn't dead. The odds piled up against him rode heavily on Ferry's shoulders.

He urged his sorrel gelding up the trail along the backbone of the ridge that drove a wedge between the two valleys, reaching out like a finger from the snow-capped mountains behind it.

The scent of pine and spruce was heavy in the air, and there was a peaceful babble of birds. But Ferry knew it was all false. There was no peace there. There was war—war between the Triangle F and the Leightons, one on either side of the ridge. It was a senseless war, the way he saw it. But now it was his war, whether he liked it or not.

Other *Leisure* books by Wayne C. Lee:

THE HOSTILE LAND
BLOOD ON THE PRAIRIE

The Gun Tamer

Wayne C. Lee

LEISURE BOOKS  NEW YORK CITY

A LEISURE BOOK®

March 2010

Published by special arrangement with Golden West Literary Agency.

Dorchester Publishing Co., Inc.
200 Madison Avenue
New York, NY 10016

ISBN 10: 0-8439-6339-5
ISBN 13: 978-0-8439-6339-7

The name "Leisure Books" and the stylized "L" with design are trademarks of Dorchester Publishing Co., Inc.

Printed in the United States of America.

10 9 8 7 6 5 4 3 2 1

Visit us online at www.dorchesterpub.com.

The Gun Tamer

I

Within the hour, Dan Ferry would be on the Triangle F—if he wasn't dead. The odds piled up against him rode heavily on Ferry's shoulders.

He urged his sorrel gelding up the trail along the backbone of the ridge that drove a wedge between the two valleys, reaching out like a finger from the snow-capped mountains behind it.

The scent of pine and spruce was heavy in the air, and there was a peaceful babble of birds. But Ferry knew it was all false. There was no peace there. There was war—war between the Triangle F and the Leightons, one on either side of the ridge. It was a senseless war, the way he saw it. But now it was his war, whether he liked it or not.

As he moved along the ridge, the trees thinned and

he caught glimpses of the valleys on either side. On his right the ridge dropped away into a valley scarcely half a mile wide. It was hemmed in on the far side by another timbered ridge stretching out from the mountains behind.

The valley on his left was much deeper and wider, rich in grass and almost treeless. Down there was the Triangle F, his ranch, now that Addison Ferry was dead, a victim of a bushwhacker's bullet.

Suddenly he rode into a clearing that straddled the crest of the ridge. Involuntarily he reined up, his gray eyes flashing over the open area. There was no movement, and he relaxed.

He was jumpy, he decided. No one in this country knew that old Ad Ferry's nephew was there. From the talk in Sundown, most people didn't think he would have nerve enough to come, things being as they were. Maybe, Ferry thought wryly, when he found out just how things really were, he'd wish he hadn't come.

Ferry rode on toward a huge boulder that seemed to dominate the whole clearing, blocking the trail. Then he reined up again as he realized this was the end of the trail up the ridge. It split here, one trail going down to the Triangle F on his left, the other running down to his right where part of the shed-like barn showed in the trees. That must be Leighton's Hooked J Ranch, according to what he'd heard in town.

Ferry started on toward the shade of the lone pine that struggled for existence by the rock, its roots buried deep beneath it.

His hat suddenly spun from his head and bounced in the dust as a shot shattered the quiet air. Ferry was on the point of following his hat when a sharp voice stopped him.

"Don't move, mister, if you want to live to pick up that hat."

For a long moment Ferry didn't move; then he turned in his saddle. A girl on a stocky roan had moved out from behind the big rock. Her hat was pushed back off her head, hanging by the chin strap, revealing a heavy roll of raven black hair. Her jet black eyes seemed to bore into his very soul.

But it was the gun that demanded his attention.

"Are you in the habit of greeting strangers like this?" he asked finally.

"Mister, strangers don't ride on Thunder Ridge," the girl said.

"This one did," Ferry said, realizing from what his

uncle's lawyer, H. E. Sperrel, had written him about the people there that this must be Rosanne Leighton, the youngest child and only girl in the Leighton family. He guessed her to be about two or three years younger than he was.

"I'll tell you for a fact, it isn't healthy," she said. "What's your business here?"

Ferry quickly weighed his chances. If he told Rosanne Leighton who he was, he'd never get down to the Triangle F. If that gun on him now didn't mean his finish, it would prod him down the ridge to the Leighton ranch, where other guns wouldn't be so reluctant.

"I'm looking for a job," Ferry said slowly, watching the girl's reaction.

Amusement flitted across her face and twinkled in her black eyes. "You don't look like the type of man that's being hired around here," she said. "Dudes are just in the way. Sorry I dusted you off just now, mister. But we don't take chances out here these days."

Ferry glanced down at his new boots and pants. With his new hat, now in the dust, he knew that he looked like a dude. He had thought of that when he bought the clothes and had decided that was all to the good. A stranger who could pass for a gunman would certainly invite a bullet first and question later. A dude might only arouse curiosity. If he had looked like a gun hand, there might have been a hole in his head now instead of in his hat.

"I take it your ranch is not looking for new hands," Ferry said. "Then I'll try this one." He jerked a thumb at the Triangle F.

"You ride down there and you'll probably get your head blown off," Rosanne said matter-of-factly.

Ferry frowned. "That's a pleasant thought. I heard there was a war going on over grazing rights on this ridge. But they told me the owner of the Triangle F was dead. Seems that ought to end the war."

"The war's just started, mister. Old Ad Ferry hired a gang of gun slicks, and they're still down there even if he isn't."

"I didn't notice such wonderful grazing on this ridge. Seems like a silly thing to kill people over."

"It isn't the ridge; it's—" She broke off, her eyes snapping. "Mister, you're awful nosy."

"Sorry," he said quickly.

"You'll be sorrier if you keep prying. Let me give you some advice. Turn that horse around and ride back to Sundown; then keep right on going."

"I might do that," Ferry said. "You know, they told me in town there was a girl in the Leighton family. But they didn't tell me how pretty she was."

A flush swept over her face. "Don't be too free with that kind of talk, mister. The last fellow who tried it is dead now."

"Dead?" Ferry exclaimed.

"Judd hanged him."

Ferry had expected to hear some bad things about Judd Leighton. But he hadn't expected anything like this.

"I suppose this fellow Judd hanged was a Triangle F man," Ferry said, unable to keep the sharpness out of his voice.

"He was, if that's any of your business." Suddenly she broke off, put binoculars to her eyes and looked down at the ranch below.

Ferry looked down at the Triangle F buildings where a man had just come out on the porch of the house. "This must be a mutual scouting post," he said.

"I don't come up here just for the ride," Rosanne said, taking the glasses from her eyes. "And I wouldn't advise you to do it again, either."

Ferry nodded. "Sounds like good advice. Who is that on the porch down there?"

"Steve Hayes," Rosanne said. "He's the ramrod of the Triangle F. If he sees you up here, he's liable to send a man out to put a hole in that new shirt of yours. He's that kind."

A whistle sounded from the trees down toward the Leighton ranch. Rosanne turned her horse that way.

"That's my brother, Joe," she said. "Better take my advice, mister. The trail back to town is still open. Use it."

She nudged her roan and started down the steep trail. Within a minute she was out of sight in the trees.

Ferry swung back to look at the Triangle F. The man on the porch had disappeared. Ferry dismounted and got his hat. If he'd had any doubt as to the seriousness of the war between the Triangle F and the Leightons, it had been dispelled by his meeting with Rosanne Leighton.

How was he going to put a stop to the fight? Somehow it had to be done. He couldn't accomplish a thing till it was.

The enormity of the job ahead tempted him to turn

and ride back down the trail he had come over and keep on riding as Rosanne had suggested.

Instead, he mounted and reined his horse into the steep trail leading down toward the Triangle F buildings sitting boldly out in the valley.

11

Ferry found the trail even steeper in places than it had looked from above. His sorrel moved along slowly, jolting stiff-legged over the sharpest declines. Trees crowded the trail, so thick that only an occasional splotch of sunlight broke through to dot the ground. The scent of pine and spruce was so heavy in the air that it seemed almost tangible.

Then the trees began to thin out and the trail started to level off. A rider suddenly appeared out of the last belt of trees, blocking the trail, a .45 balanced in his hand.

"That's far enough, mister."

Ferry reined up at the gravelly command and folded his hands on the pommel of the saddle. The man he was facing was a short stocky fellow with several days' growth of beard on his face.

"I'm not arguing," Ferry said.

"Wish you would," the man grunted. "That would make it easier. What was you doing up on the ridge?"

"I came out from town that way," Ferry said. "Any law against that?"

"Maybe. People don't ride along the ridge to look at the scenery any more. And they sure don't meet up with that Leighton filly just to pass the time of day."

"You saw me talking to the Leighton girl?"

"We ain't blind down here. Anybody friendly to the Leightons ain't likely to be welcome on this side of the ridge. I'm taking you in to the boss."

"Good," Ferry said, and his relief was genuine. He didn't like the look in the dirty man's face. "I came out here to see Steve Hayes."

"What do you want to see Hayes about?" the man demanded suspiciously.

"I'll tell him."

"You'll do it with my gun in your ribs." The man motioned toward the house. "Any funny moves and you won't be telling anybody anything."

Ferry rode out on the grassy floor of the valley with the gunman just behind him. The ranch buildings were only a quarter of a mile from the base of the ridge. The freshly peeled logs in the corral, gleaming in the sun, seemed to be the only new or striking improvement on the place.

The house was a large rambling structure with a long veranda running the length of it. Another smaller building, apparently a bunkhouse, stood only a few feet from the house. The two barns were badly in need of repair. A swiftly moving stream charged out of the valley to the west and cut through one corner of the corral.

Ferry let his horse choose the pace and, when they reached the hitchrail, dismounted without an order from the gunman.

"Hey, Steve," the man yelled, "I brought in the jasper."

The call brought a line of men through the door onto the veranda. The leader, a tall muscular man with sandy hair and pale blue eyes that appeared at first glance to be almost colorless, looked Ferry over from head to foot with deliberate scorn. Then he turned to the gunman who had brought Ferry in.

"Why didn't you beef him like I told you to? He was talking to the Leighton girl. That proves whose side he is on."

"I figured to," the man said. "But I hired out to fight. There ain't no fight in this jasper. He says he wants to see you."

"Better dehorn him just in case he suddenly decides he is a scrapper," Hayes said. "Then bring him in."

The foreman spun on his heel and strode back inside. The gunman reached over and took Ferry's .45, then prodded him into the house.

"Now what do you want?" Hayes demanded, dropping into a chair facing Ferry.

Ferry pulled a chair over and sat down. "Maybe I'd better tell you who I am first."

"It might help."

"My name is Dan Ferry."

"Ferry?" Hayes left his chair as if it had exploded under him. "Suffering Jupiter! Are you old Ad's nephew?"

Ferry nodded. "I am. Didn't you expect me to come?"

"No," Hayes said. "Sperrel said you might. But we sure ain't been looking forward to it."

"I didn't expect you to bring out a brass band to

welcome me," Ferry said grimly. "But I'm here now. I own this ranch. You're working for me. Whether you like it or not makes no difference to me."

"I don't figure on liking it," Hayes said.

"You can quit any time," Ferry said.

A mirthless grin split the foreman's face. "We're not liable to give up a hundred a month to ride the grub line. And you can't fire us for six months. I happen to know that."

Ferry nodded. "That's what Sperrel wrote me. Old Ad had crazy ideas. Since you won't quit and I can't fire you, we'd better make the best of it. Now I want to hear your version of this whole mess."

Hayes looked at the four men lounging on the cot and some chairs before he turned to Ferry. Ferry looked at the men, too. There was no mistaking the hard brand of the gunman on three of the four faces.

The fourth man was little more than a youngster, and he had the mischievous grin of a boy on his face right now. The way he carried his gun spoke of his profession, but Ferry felt that his face revealed a side of him that the other men in this room didn't have.

"If you want my opinion," Hayes said deliberately, "it's going to be some scrap."

"I want to hear what you know about it," Ferry said. "What started it?"

"I can't rightly say about that," Hayes said. "There was plenty of bad blood between the Leightons and the old man when Ad hired me. He told me to get together a crew that could hold its own against anything the Leightons could throw at us. I reckon I did just that."

Ferry looked over the men again and nodded in agreement. "Did you know you were getting into a feud?"

"Sure," Hayes said. "I'm not about to punch cows for a living. And neither are these boys."

"Do you know what the fight is all about?"

"Not exactly," Hayes said. "The old man hired us to fight, and that's what we do. We ain't asking questions."

Ferry nodded slowly. These were hired killers; nothing more. And according to his uncle's will, he couldn't fire them for six months. Anything could happen in that time.

"How about this fellow that Judd Leighton hanged?" Ferry asked. "He was one of your crew, wasn't he?"

The foreman's face clouded. "That was Charlie

Davis. I made a mistake hiring him. He was handy with a gun, all right. But he thought he was handy with the women, too. He got sweet on the Leighton girl. Reckon he deserved to get his neck stretched for not showing any better sense than that."

"Sounds like Rosanne Leighton is poison," Ferry said.

"She is to anybody from over here. Judd and the twins, Jule and Jake, caught Charlie coming home from town one day. He was out by the Bradford ranch on the ridge trail, probably aiming to meet Rosanne on the ridge. The Leightons accused Charlie of rustling some of their cattle and packed him off to their ranch.

"Hugh Bradford pounded leather to tell us, and we rode over the ridge to the Hooked J as fast as we could. But we were too late. Charlie was dangling from a tree limb in their yard when we got there. We couldn't save Charlie, but we dusted them off a little with lead."

"Kill anybody?"

"Guess not. Winged old man Leighton. That ought to keep him from fighting."

"And after that?"

"Nothing's happened since. But things figure to pop loose tonight at the dance."

"Any special reason?" Ferry asked.

Hayes grinned. "I'm taking Mamie to the dance to-night. And Judd ain't going to like that."

Ferry thought of asking who Mamie was but decided against it. She was obviously a bone of contention between Steve Hayes and Judd Leighton. His problem now was to put an end to the feud one way or another.

"You're drawing good money for this job, aren't you?" he asked.

"Sure," Hayes said carelessly. "A hundred a month. Forty is the best a man can do punching cows. But the old man could afford it. He had plenty."

"Where did he get it?"

Hayes shrugged. "He was your uncle; not mine. He was gone from the ranch almost every day, sometimes for two or three days at a stretch. I reckon he got his money on those trips. He made it plain we were paid to fight and not ask questions."

"How would you like to draw a hundred a month and not do any fighting?"

The foreman's mouth fell open, and a wave of startled exclamations and oaths traveled along the row of men behind him. The youngster recovered his voice first.

"What in blazes are you driving at, boss?"

"I intend to stop this senseless fighting if possible. Any objections?"

"Plenty," Hayes said angrily, his colorless eyes glaring at Ferry. "Maybe we weren't caring how the fight went when we first took this job. But we've got a personal interest now. We're not going to let the Leightons get away with some of the high-handed things they've pulled."

"What things?" Ferry demanded.

"Such as hanging Charlie Davis," Hayes said. "He wasn't much, maybe, but he was one of our boys. And the Leightons are going to pay for that."

Ferry looked at the other four men. "That how you feel, too?"

"Reckon so," the youngster said. "We'll back Steve."

The other three nodded in agreement. Ferry turned back to face the foreman.

"You're overlooking one thing, Hayes," he said, his jaw set. "Maybe I can't fire you. But I'm boss here. I'll give the orders. And those orders are to avoid any fight with the Leightons if you can. I've got work to do here that can't be done until this feud is ended."

"If you're so all-fired set on getting this fight over," Hayes said sarcastically, "you'd better oil up that gun of yours and pitch in and help end it. That's the only way it will ever be settled—in gunsmoke."

Ferry got up. "We'll try it my way first, he said.

Hayes got up so fast he knocked his chair backward. "All right! Get yourself killed if that's what you want! Me and the boys will be ready. Any time the Leightons want a scrap, they won't have to beg us. Slim, show our peace-loving boss around the place. Maybe he'd like to see it before the Leightons tear it apart."

"Sure thing," the youngster said. "Come on, boss. I'll show you the kitchen first. It's the most important room around here."

As Ferry started after the youngster, the man who had taken his gun held it out to him, a sullen frown on his face. Ferry took it without a word. It wasn't hard to see how he stood with his crew. They had no respect for a tenderfoot, and they made no effort to hide the fact that they thought he was just that. They resented his orders. Ferry doubted if they would make even a pretense of following them.

Slim, though, was different. He didn't seem to resent anything, not even his new boss. He was like a happy boy, willing to accept things as they came as long as they didn't interfere with his enjoyment of life.

The kitchen was the room next to the one they had been in. Slim had stopped there. Ferry ran his eyes over the shelves along one side of the room, with pots and pans hanging under the shelves. A huge stove with a box partly filled with wood cut into stove lengths was in the far end of the room. Working over a table in the middle of the floor was a Chinese, his queue flopping back and forth across his back as he scurried around.

"Here, Golly Gee," Slim said, "meet your new boss."

The Chinese looked up, his face spread in a wide grin. "Wong Ling velly glad see bossy man." He frowned at Slim. "Name Wong Ling. Not Golly Gee."

"Looks like this outfit has a good cook, anyway," Ferry said.

"Golly Gee is the best cook in the Rockies," Slim said.

"Name not Golly Gee," the Chinese protested vigorously. "Name Wong Ling."

Slim laughed and led Ferry into another room. "Your bedroom," he said, jerking a thumb at a partition door. "Say, I don't recall us being properly introduced. I'm Slim Walters. I'm mighty glad to see you, even if some of the rest of the boys aren't."

Ferry felt his instant liking for this boy growing by leaps and bounds. He instinctively saw an ally in Slim.

"How old are you, Slim?" he asked.

"Twenty," Slim said. "A lot of people think I'm younger. A few men have made the mistake of taking me for a kid." His hand darted down, and suddenly Ferry was looking into the bore of Slim's .45. "They didn't make that mistake twice. Nor any other mistake."

Ferry stared at Slim. "You don't look like you belonged in this business."

Slim grinned and shrugged. "Why not? A man uses the tools he's been given. I was given fast hands. And my dad gave me a gun when I was six. There's no tool I can use better than this. Why shouldn't I make a soft living with it if I can? And I can."

"You said you were glad to see me come," Ferry said. "Don't you like taking orders from Steve Hayes?"

Slim shrugged again. "Steve's all right so long as he uses his head. I liked the way you stood him on his ear in there." He grinned. "Steve gets too big for his boots now and then. You're the boss and you told him so. I hope you make it stick."

Ferry studied the young gunman's face. "You think I can't?"

Slim spread his hands. "I didn't say that. But—well, look, boss. You're a tenderfoot. Your clothes show that. That law spieler, Sperrel, told us you'd been in college. This ain't exactly a college out here. Naturally the boys ain't going to respect you. But like I told you, I liked the way you stood up to Steve. I think you've got the backbone even if you lack the know-how."

Ferry nodded. He had to like Slim's honesty and frankness. He was going to need an ally in this crew. Slim was his only chance for that. The quicker he formed that alliance, the better off he'd be.

As Slim led the way from the house across the ten-foot alley to the bunkhouse, Ferry decided to take the plunge. Once inside the bunkhouse, he confronted Slim.

"You seem to be willing to take my orders instead

of Hayes',," Ferry said. "Would you be willing to keep those orders confidential? The rest of the crew is obviously going to listen to Hayes."

"Sure, boss," Slim said unhesitatingly.

"In the first place, my name is Dan Ferry, not boss. In the second place, I'm not the tenderfoot you think. I've been to college, all right, but that was two years ago. I've been punching cows in Wyoming since then. I wanted to look like a greenhorn because I thought that gave me my best chance to get out here and get the lay of the land without stopping a bullet."

Slim grinned. "Smart thinking. Maybe college learning does pay off. Are you handy with that shooting iron?"

"I can shoot well enough," Ferry said. "I belonged to a pistol team in college. But I can't handle the gun like an expert, if that's what you mean."

"It is," Slim said. "I reckon you'd better learn to get that thing clear of leather in a hurry. Straight shooting won't help you if your gun's still in your holster."

"I'm more interested in getting this senseless fight stopped," Ferry said. "Who is this Mamie Steve Hayes is taking to the dance tonight and why is that going to cause trouble?"

"She's a percentage girl," Slim said. "Works at Ned Sailer's Silver Spur Saloon. She gets off Saturday nights to go to the regular dance at the hall. Sometimes she goes with Judd Leighton; sometimes with Steve. Tonight it's Steve."

"And that means trouble?" Ferry said.

"What else? Mamie's been leading on Both Steve and Judd, hoping they'll fight over her. I figure tonight's the night she'll make it work. This is the first dance since the Leightons hung Charlie Davis. We owe them something for that."

"So you're all going, looking for a fight?"

"We'll be there, heeled and ready, just in case."

"I've got different ideas," Ferry said. "But I'll need your help. How about it?"

Slim stared at Ferry for a moment. "I've got a hunch I ain't going to like this. But you're the boss. What's on your mind?"

"I have good reasons for trying to stop this fight as soon as possible. Nobody but you fellows here on the ranch know who I am. Can I depend on you to keep it that way?"

Slim nodded, grinning. "Sure. Steve and the boys

ain't about to admit a tenderfoot is their boss. Are you figuring on stopping the fracas at the dance tonight?"

"If it comes to a fight and I can see a way to keep it from getting out of hand, I intend to try. Will you back me?"

Slim shrugged. "I said I would. I don't go back on my word. But I figure we're more likely to stop lead than the fight."

"You don't have to help," Ferry said.

Slim grinned. "I figure it's going to be a fight either way. I'll just side you and see what happens."

"I've got some business in town," Ferry said. "I'll ride back in now."

"Too bad you won't get to sample Golly Gee's cooking. We'd better tell him."

Ferry followed Slim back across the alley between the house and the bunkhouse and into the kitchen. As Slim went through the partition door, he bumped into the Chinese cook crossing the room with a tin cupful of flour. The cup bounced out of the cook's hand, spraying flour over the floor.

"Golly gee! Golly gee!" the Chinaman exploded,

gazing at the mess.

"Sorry, Golly Gee," Slim said. "We just came in to tell you the boss won't be here for supper. Want me to get down and lick up that flour?"

The cook didn't reply. He picked up the cup and started for the broom in the corner. "Golly gee!" he muttered again.

Slim laughed. "See where he gets his name, Dan? That's the limit of his cussing. They say the first English words a foreigner picks up are cuss words. I'd like to know where Golly Gee landed. The old man had him here when we came."

They left the Chinese to his cleaning and went into the main room. The men were still lounging there.

"I'll be at the dance tonight," Ferry announced. "So far as you men are concerned, you've never seen me before. Is that clear?"

"Plain as poison," Hayes said. "You're just a dude we don't know. We like it that way."

Ferry went on out to his horse, and Slim followed.

"I'll put your bedroll in the house," Slim offered. "Might be a good idea to have your horse hitched close to the hall tonight." He grinned. "I've made it a rule never to start a fight against big odds without having a saddled horse handy."

Ferry was filled with misgivings as he rode out of the yard.

III

Sundown could boast of little more than two rows of buildings, some badly in need of repair, that lined the dusty road for a couple of hundred yards. The dozen business establishments were huddled together in the center of town like chickens frightened by a hawk. Homes were at either end of the street, with a few scattered haphazardly behind the business houses.

Dan Ferry rode cautiously into town for the second time that day. He reined up at the hitchrail in front of the hotel. He'd stopped there before and asked for H. E. Sperrel. But the clerk had said the lawyer wasn't in. He crossed the wide porch and went into the small lobby. He asked the rotund clerk if Sperrel was in.

"Yep," the clerk replied instantly. "Room 18. I told him there was a stranger inquiring for him. He went right to his room and has been there ever since. Reckon he must be powerful anxious to see you."

The clerk waited expectantly for Ferry to explain things more fully, but Ferry only thanked him and hurried up the stairs.

Ferry found Room 18 and knocked. Almost instantly the door opened and a small wiry man invited him inside.

"I've been looking for you ever since the clerk said a stranger had inquired for me," Sperrel said. "Where have you been?"

"Out at the Triangle F," Ferry said. "I met Rosanne Leighton on the ridge that runs between the Triangle F and the valley to the north."

The lawyer puckered his lips in a silent whistle. "You've really been stretching your luck. Rosanne Leighton is pretty and she may look harmless. But she's as handy with that gun of hers as most men. She isn't afraid to use it, either."

"She convinced me of that," Ferry said, showing the lawyer the bullet hole in his new hat.

Sperrel whistled audibly. "She could have put that through your skull instead of your hat if she had wanted to." He spun a chair around for Ferry, then seated himself on the edge of the bed. "I wasn't sure you'd come. I tried to make it clear in my letter that you'd be stepping into an inferno."

Ferry felt the lawyer's bright eyes weighing him, testing him. There was something about the little man that suggested the paradox of sudden lightning and a slow deliberation born of shrewd calculation.

"You made it clear," Ferry said. "But you also sounded as though you wanted me to come if I could."

"I did," the lawyer said. "Old Ad's will left the entire Triangle F Ranch to you. But he made it plain that I was to remain here and see that his crew got paid and the ranch stayed in your name until you did come to take over. Needless to say, I have no desire to stay here indefinitely, especially in the middle of this range war."

"Now that I'm here, you can go East. Is that it?"

Sperrel nodded. "That's right. But I've got a few things to tell you before I do. First, you inherited more than just a ranch, you know. You inherited that crew of men out there. For six months you can't fire them. And you must stay on the ranch for one year or you lose it, too."

"You told me that in your letter. I can understand

why my uncle wanted me to stay on the ranch for a year to claim it. But why do I have to keep those gunslingers around? If I could get rid of them, surely I could settle any differences with the Leightons."

Sperrel took out a cigar and lighted it. "You didn't learn much on that ride out there, did you? The Leightons are not about to sign a peace treaty with anybody named Ferry. Don't forget that. That's why Ad demanded that you keep those gun hands on the ranch. They're for your protection. Besides, there is a lot more at stake than just the ranch. You know about the mine, don't you?"

"Sure," Ferry said. "Ad wrote me once—about two months ago. He said he had a mine and it was making him a fortune. He didn't give any details. He never did write much, you know."

Sperrel nodded. "How well I know! Getting information from him was like prying a turtle out of its shell. I thought maybe he had written more to you."

"He didn't. I was hoping you could fill me in."

"I don't know very much about it," Sperrel said. "That mine apparently is a rich one, judging from the way Ad's bank account blossomed after he got his hands on it. I know that it's the real source of trouble between the Triangle F and the Leightons."

"I figured that. Only a bunch of idiots would start a shooting war over the grazing rights to Thunder Ridge. Where is the mine?"

"That's just it," Sperrel said. "Nobody knows."

"What?" Ferry ejaculated. "Ad had a partner. Somebody must know."

Sperrel shook his head. "I don't think so. The Leightons, however, apparently think somebody, or maybe everybody, over on the Triangle F knows where it is. They intend to find out if they have to kill everybody on the Triangle F to do it. I think that is the whole thing boiled down to the simplest terms."

"And nobody knows anything to tell even if he wanted to."

Sperrel got up and walked to the window and looked down on the street. "That's about it. Ad wrote me after his partner was killed that he was the only man alive who knew where the mine was. If he had been going to tell anyone, I'm sure I would have been the one. Your uncle and I were life-long friends. After he came West, I still did all his legal business. His trouble with the Leightons over grazing rights to Thunder Ridge wouldn't have amounted to much, I'm sure, if it hadn't been for the mine.

"That all started about three years ago, although nobody suspected it then. An old prospector by the name of Jig Ailey came by the Triangle F one day. Ad, in one of his soft moments, grub-staked the old fellow. About eight months ago, Ad wrote me that Ailey had struck a rich pocket. Ailey was getting old and couldn't work the mine alone, so he made Ad a fifty-fifty partner."

The lawyer paused, and Ferry waited patiently for him to continue.

"Ad wrote that the mine was somewhere behind the Triangle F in a place called Secret Valley. In later letters he told of growing troubles with the Leightons. It seems the Leightons were getting suspicious of Ad's sudden wealth and curious about where he was getting it. Knowing Ad as I did, I don't doubt that he flaunted his riches in their faces. He had a conceited streak in him and liked to crow over his enemies.

"Things started coming to a head when Jig Ailey was murdered. Ad said he had been tortured, apparently in an attempt to make him tell where the mine was located. Ailey's death left the mine entirely to Ad. Ad suspected the Leightons of the murder, and he was sure he was next on the list. That's when he hired Steve Hayes and ordered him to round up a crew of gun hands."

"Getting the gunmen didn't keep Ad from being killed," Ferry said.

"No, it didn't," Sperrel admitted. "There were peculiar circumstances leading up to and surrounding Ad's death. Shortly after Jig Ailey was killed, Matt Lundo, a brother of Mrs. Leighton, began following Ad. Ad wrote me about it. He said Lundo was the meanest man he had ever seen. Ad thought Lundo was just waiting to locate the mine before killing him. The last letter I got from Ad said that Lundo had followed him to Secret Valley one day. Ad had spotted him and there had been a running fight. On Thunder Ridge, just above the Leighton ranch, Ad got in a lucky shot and killed Lundo.

"Judd Leighton swore he'd kill Ad. Ad wrote that he wasn't leaving the ranch any oftener than was absolutely necessary any more. He sent me directions how to get to Secret Valley."

Sperrel unfolded a letter he took from his brief case and read slowly:

" 'To get to Secret Valley, just follow Thunder

Ridge to its source. That's about fifteen miles above the ranch, I calculate. You'll find the water coming out of a hole in the rocks like a big spring. It's really an underground river coming to the surface. Close by you'll find a trough worn in the canyon wall ages ago by running water. Go up this trough. It's steep, but a horse can make it. Follow this trough and you'll come into Secret Valley.' "

The lawyer looked up. "He also says here that anybody who didn't know the trough was a trail would never find the way into Secret Valley."

"What about the mine itself?" Ferry asked.

The lawyer shrugged. "I wish I knew. He promised to tell me how to find it the next time he wrote. I don't know why he didn't put the directions in this letter."

"Where is that other letter?"

"It never came. Evidently Ad was killed before he got it written."

"You said there were peculiar circumstances surrounding Ad's death," Ferry said. "I never heard anything except what you wrote me."

"Well, the way I understand it, Ad was killed on Thunder Ridge at night. He was alone—none of the gunmen he had hired was with him. Now what was he doing on Thunder Ridge at night? Something about that just doesn't make sense. I don't think there is any doubt that it was Judd Leighton who killed him. Judd had made threats openly. And I've heard he even bragged later that he had killed him."

"I suppose you think I should live by the 'eye for an eye' code and go after Judd Leighton," Ferry said.

The lawyer shook his head. "I'm a lawyer, not an executioner. It seems to me it would be to your advantage to stop the fighting if you can and find the mine."

"That's exactly what I intend to do, if possible," Ferry said. "Has there been much fighting since Ad was killed?"

"The only real clash, I think, was the day Judd hanged Charlie Davis, a Triangle F man," Sperrel said. "The Triangle F crew rode over and there was a pretty lively skirmish, the way I hear it. But the Leightons are eager to get their fingers on that mine. They'll keep at it till they get it or are licked, and a lot of people will probably be killed in the process."

"This Connie Bradden you mentioned in your letter is about the only person alive who has been in Secret Valley, isn't she?" Ferry asked.

"I think so," the lawyer said. "She got lost up in that valley behind the Triangle F one day, and Jig Ailey, the soft-hearted old fool, took her into Secret Valley with him. She kept house for him until he was killed. That wasn't more than a week or two. She told me she didn't find out where the mine was. She works in that restaurant right across the street from this hotel."

"I know," Ferry said. "When I didn't find you here this morning, I went over there for something to eat. I found out who the waitress was, got real friendly and made a date with her for the dance tonight."

The lawyer showed his surprise. "You move fast, don't you?"

"Only when I think it necessary. From what you said in your letter, I thought Connie Bradden might be able to tell me some of the things I want to know."

"I'm afraid Connie won't be much help. But you can ask." Sperrel started putting papers back into his brief case. "I don't know of anything else I can do to help you. You understand the terms of the will. The Triangle F is yours only if you stay there a year. And you can't fire your present crew for six months. You'll probably understand the wisdom of that as the days go by. My job was to stay here, pay the crew and keep an eye on things till you arrived. I guess I'm relieved of my duties now. I'm going back East tomorrow."

Ferry stood up to leave. "I doubt if there will be any peace along Thunder Ridge until I can get rid of Steve Hayes and those gunmen. It's going to be tough, looking for a mine with a war going on."

Sperrel nodded. "You're right about that. But you must find that mine."

"How am I going to do that if it's as well hidden as Ad indicated?"

"Perhaps he left a map or some kind of directions for you somewhere. Ad had queer ideas, you know. Since he didn't send me the letter telling how to find the mine, perhaps he made some arrangements to put instructions directly in your hands when you got here. I hope so. Anyway, I wish you luck. You'll need it."

Ferry went out the door.

IV

Dan Ferry paused on the veranda of the hotel. It was almost sundown. It wouldn't be long before it was time to pick up Connie and walk her to the town hall for the dance. If he didn't get some answers from her, he'd be faced with the almost impossible task of trying to find a hidden mine on one hand and fighting a war on the other.

When Ferry went into the restaurant, he saw Connie behind the counter close to the kitchen door, and one glance told him she was practically ready for the dance. Although she wore a big apron, it didn't completely cover her frilly white dress, and it did nothing to distract from the flashing blue eyes and high-piled blonde hair. Right now there was a bright flush in her cheeks that Ferry didn't remember seeing earlier.

A short heavy-set man about Ferry's age was leaning far over the counter talking earnestly to Connie. His unruly reddish-brown hair stood up like a brush, giving the impression of an abnormally long head. His heavy features seemed twisted in his beefy face by a broken nose that had grown together crooked, giving his face a peculiar flat look. The baleful gleam in his yellowish-green eyes reminded Ferry of the glare of an angry cat.

"I've told you all I know, Link Dalton," Connie said in a low, tight voice. "Now let me alone."

"You know more," the man snapped. "And you're going to tell me."

He reached across the counter and grabbed Connie's arm, pulling her halfway over the counter.

Ferry didn't wait for any more.

With a few swift strides, he crossed the room. Something in Connie's eyes must have warned the man, for he turned quickly, releasing Connie's wrist. But he wasn't in time to avoid Ferry's hands as Ferry grabbed the man's shirt and jerked him away from the counter.

"You heard the lady," Ferry snapped. "Leave her alone!"

Dalton tried to knock Ferry's hands away. "Keep

your nose out of this!"

"It's already in and it's staying in," Ferry said. "Are you going to get out or shall I throw you out?"

Dalton's thick lips split in a sneer. "Try it, mister."

A surge of anger swept over Ferry, and he wheeled the heavy man around and shoved him toward the door. Dalton backed a few steps until he caught his balance. Then he lunged at Ferry.

But Ferry was expecting that. Instead of giving ground, he moved forward to meet the charge, smashing a fist into the beefy face. Blood spurted from the flattened nose and an oath hissed through the thick lips.

Dalton lunged forward recklessly, landing a blow that rocked Ferry back against a table. Ferry rolled off the table onto his feet, however, before Dalton could follow up his advantage.

Ferry retreated, waiting for Dalton to make another wild charge. He was sure now that was the way the redhead would fight. Ferry bumped into a table, and Dalton chose that moment to make another lunge at him.

Ferry sidestepped and drove two stinging blows to the redhead's face. Dalton bellowed and wheeled to face Ferry. It was then that Ferry lowered his blows, catching Dalton just under the ribs.

Dalton doubled up, and Ferry straightened him with a hard fist to the jaw. He stumbled back, catching a heel on a chair leg, then staggered almost to the door, trying desperately to regain his balance. But at the door, Ferry caught him flush on the jaw with a fist that had all his strength behind it.

Dalton reeled back through the door and across the small porch. For an instant he teetered on the edge of the porch; then he sprawled under the hitchrack. His horse, tied to the bar, lunged back to the end of its reins.

With a smothered oath, Dalton clawed for his gun. But Ferry was on the porch, and he leaped down, planting a foot on Dalton's wrist, and with his other boot kicked the gun away. The horse reared back, breaking its reins, and galloped down the street.

"Get up and catch your horse and clear out," Ferry said.

Dalton got up, wiping a sleeve across his bloody face. "There'll be another time, mister. Just don't forget that."

He started to pick up his gun, but Ferry stopped

him.

"Leave it! It will still be there after you've caught your horse."

Ferry wheeled and walked back into the restaurant. Connie was standing just inside the door, her face drained of color.

"You've made a very dangerous enemy, Mr. Forbes," she said.

He stared at Connie. For a moment, he had forgotten he had given her a false name earlier.

"I seem to have several enemies here," he said dryly, "most of them ready made. It's sort of nice to have one I made myself."

Connie stared at him. "I'm glad you're happy about it. I wouldn't be."

"Maybe it's just that when a man tries to kill me, I like to know why he's doing it," Ferry said. "If Dalton tries it now, at least I'll know why. Isn't it about time to head for the dance?"

"I'm ready if you are," Connie said.

"I'd like to take the long way to the hall," Ferry said. "I've got some questions to ask you."

She looked at him doubtfully. "I'm not promising to answer. Link Dalton had some questions, too."

"I promise not to be as insistent as Dalton was," Ferry said quickly, realizing he had blundered by mentioning questions, and hoping he could quiet her suspicions. If she refused to tell him anything, his real purpose in taking her to the dance would be defeated.

Outside the restaurant, Connie turned away from the town hall and around the corner into a dusty street that quickly dwindled to a trail which followed the bank of Sundown River.

The trail wound among some trees that grew next to the water. Here Ferry stopped. "I want to ask you some questions, Connie. If you don't want to answer, I guess there's nothing I can do about it. How much did you know about Jig Ailey and his mine up in Secret Valley?"

Connie's eyes widened as she stared at Ferry. "How did you know about Jig Ailey and his mine?"

"I know several things you probably don't think I do. But I must find out more. I know you kept house for Jig Ailey up in the valley."

"But like Link Dalton, you want to know where the mine is. Right?"

"So that's what Dalton wanted to know," Ferry said

in surprise. "How did he know about that?"

"Maybe the same way you learned, Mr. Forbes." Connie's tone was icy. "If you want me to tell you anything, you'll have to give me some good reason why I should."

"That's fair enough," Ferry said after a moment's consideration. "I'll start by telling you my name isn't Forbes; it's Dan Ferry."

"Ferry?" she gasped, her hand flying to her mouth, almost smothering the word. There was no mistaking the fear in her face.

"Am I poison just because my name is Ferry?" he asked.

"No, it isn't that," she said quickly, a wave of crimson sweeping into her face. "I was just surprised."

Ferry had seen more than surprise recorded in her face. "Now you know why I want to find out about Jig Ailey and the mine he and Ad Ferry had. Will you tell me anything?"

"I'm afraid I can't tell you much," Connie said, regaining her composure. "I never saw the mine. Jig Ailey didn't offer to tell me about it, and I didn't ask. He was a nice old man, and he treated me fine. He spent most of his time either in his bedroom or down by the river panning."

"Maybe he panned the gold out of the river."

"Maybe," Connie said. "But I got curious enough to try my luck one day. I don't know much about gold, but I'm sure there's nothing worth panning in that stream."

"Did Ad Ferry come up to see Ailey often?"

"Several times. But they usually just went into Mr. Ailey's bedroom, where they could talk in private, and spent the time there. Really, Mr. Ferry, I don't have the slightest idea where the mine is or even if there is one."

Ferry couldn't question her sincerity.

"Do any of the Leightons know how to get to Secret Valley?" he asked.

"I don't think so. As far as I know, I'm the only one who knows, unless your uncle left directions for you."

"He did," Ferry said. He glanced at the shadows moving down from the mountains to swallow up the town. "It's time to go on to the dance. But now that you know who I am, maybe you'd rather not go."

"How many people know who you are?" Connie asked.

"Nobody but the Triangle F crew. And they promised not to tell."

She smiled. "I'll take a chance then. You've been honest with me, Dan. I'd better be honest with you. Didn't you wonder why I agreed to this date with a total stranger?"

"A little," Ferry admitted. "But I just chalked it up to my good luck."

"I've got a problem of my own. Joe Leighton, the youngest of the four Leighton boys, asked me to go to the dance with him. He's a nice fellow, not like his brothers. But I knew there would be trouble if I went with him, so I told him I had other plans. Then Slim Walters, one of your men, asked me. I told him the same. When you came along, it was almost like an answer to a prayer."

Ferry grinned. "It certainly looks like we were meant to go to the dance together tonight. So let's go."

They walked on along the trail, turning presently into one that led back to the main street between the bank and a feed store. The town hall was just across the street from the bank.

Lanterns were being lighted and hung from the low ceiling when Ferry and Connie reached the door. Already the hitching rack in front of the hall was half full of saddled horses. Several teams were hitched to the bar that ran along the side of the building.

Tension hung like a cloud inside the hall. Three musicians were on a platform, but they were making no preparations to start playing, although the hall was over half full.

"Why doesn't the dance start?" Ferry asked.

A man at Ferry's elbow answered, "Because nobody's here yet, mister."

Ferry nodded. He understood what the man meant. A few minutes later, some of the important people everyone was waiting for arrived. The crowd parted as if a wedge had been driven into it, and Judd Leighton stalked into the opening, followed by his brothers, the twins, Jule and Jake, and Joe. Three other men were with them. All wore guns in tied-down holsters.

"Looks like an army," Ferry whispered to Connie.

"It is," Connie said. "I hear Steve Hayes is bringing Mamie tonight. If he does, there will be a battle."

"Not if I can help it," Ferry said grimly.

Another commotion focused all attention on the door. Again the crowd parted, forming a lane so the newcomers could reach the enter of the room. This time it was the Triangle F crew. Steve Hayes led the parade, a flaxen-haired woman at his side. Her pale blue eyes were beaming up at her escort in a show of rapt admiration. The hard cast of her face added years to her appearance. Ferry guessed she was really some-where in her early twenties, although she might easily have passed for thirty.

Ferry glanced at Judd Leighton and saw the dark scowl on his face. Trouble wouldn't have to beckon hard to get a response from him. The musicians, ap-parently satisfied that everyone of importance was present, started playing, and the crowd turned almost reluctantly to the business of dancing.

Ferry reached out his hand to Connie. "Shall we?"

She smiled. "That's what we came for, isn't it?"

"Partly." Ferry, watching Mamie, saw her flash a big smile at Judd. "Looks like real trouble coming tonight."

Connie nodded. "Mamie will try to get Steve and Judd to fight if she can. And I think she can. Look at Judd."

Judd was elbowing his way toward Steve Hayes and Mamie, a heavy scowl on his face. Hayes had an equally dark frown when he stepped back as Judd cut in. Ferry could practically feel the tension that gripped the room as people watched expectantly.

The music stopped, and Hayes went back to claim Mamie for the next dance. The music had barely started again when Connie called Ferry's attention to the Triangle F foreman and Mamie, almost in the center of the room.

Ferry looked. Hayes was saying something to Mamie, and it obviously wasn't a compliment. Mamie stopped suddenly and jerked away from Hayes, her strident voice raised to a pitch that carried through the entire room.

"I'll dance with anybody I please, Steve Hayes. Just put that in your pipe and smoke it!"

Everything came to an abrupt breathless halt. The musicians stopped in the middle of a strain, the fiddler's last note ending in a dying wail as the bow slid off the string.

Judd lumbered toward the center of the room with an amazing alacrity for one of his size. The women scurried for neutral corners. Only Mamie held her ground, hurling defiance at Hayes.

Almost before he realized it, Ferry found himself in a circle of men that enclosed Steve Hayes and Judd.

Ranging next to him were the Triangle F men with Slim at the far end. Facing them across the circle were the Leightons and their men.

Judd quickly took up the argument, and Mamie slipped out of the circle, a triumphant smirk on her face.

"You heard what Mamie said!" Judd's heavy voice rumbled. "She'll dance with anyone she wants to. And that means me!"

Hayes' nostrils flared. "Who I tell her she can dance with is none of your business."

"I'll make it my business!" Judd's huge frame dropped into a crouch.

"Let's see you try it!"

The challenge had been hurled. Hands poised like claws above gun butts. Hayes' slate-colored eyes locked with Judd's jet black ones, each man trying to catch that telltale flicker that would warn him that his enemy was about to draw.

Time seemed to be suspended. Around the circle, every eye was on the two men in the center, hands hovering close to guns. Ferry had a second to make his move—no more—and he knew it. While all eyes remained glued on the drama in the center of the circle, his hand slipped down and brought up his gun. No one noticed.

"Stop it!" he snapped, shattering the tension as effectively as a rifle shot.

He had been almost too late. Hands had suddenly darted for guns. Now they froze at the unexpected command. Ferry, eyeing the two in the circle, saw his foreman's hand gripping his gun while Judd's gun was already part way out of the holster.

A movement across the circle caught Ferry's eye. But it stopped as Slim said softly, "I wouldn't."

Slim, grinning like a youngster at a picnic, had his gun in his hand, and it seemed to cover the entire Leighton faction. The hand that had dropped to a gun butt eased away from it.

The men, who had hesitated momentarily at Ferry's unexpected interference, had been willing to take a chance on the stranger's ability to back up his order with his gun. But when Slim took a hand, all gambling ceased. Slim's gun was not an unknown quality.

"Now raise your hands gentle like," Slim said softly, enjoyment in his voice.

Dozens of hands slowly reached toward the ceiling.

"That looks nice," Slim said. He flipped a glance at

Ferry. "What now, mister?"

Ferry looked over the men. "Hayes," he said, "take your men and go home."

Hayes swore. "This ain't none of—"

"Ride!"

Ferry's eyes bored into his foreman. Hayes' hands started lowering; his face was white with rage. "I'll go when I get ready!"

"I reckon you're ready now," Slim said, barely controlling his bubbling laughter. "This way out."

Hayes choked back words that gurgled in his throat, then stalked blindly out the door, followed by all the Triangle F crew except Slim. Judd watched them go, then turned blazing eyes on Ferry.

"You'll pay for this, mister!" he warned.

"Did you want to get half your men killed?" Ferry demanded, meeting Judd's blazing eyes without flinching.

"We can take care of ourselves without any help from a pin-eared dude!" Judd's face turned purple. "If I ever get my hands on you I'll break every bone in your body. That's a promise!"

"And how about me?" Slim asked quietly.

Judd whirled, beside himself with rage at the taunt

in Slim's voice. "I'll tear your heart out!"

Slim grinned. "Sounds interesting. Don't figure on trying it now, do you?"

The grin faded from Slim's face. Ferry saw a new light there, bright and feverish. It wasn't by chance that Slim had gotten the reputation of a gunman.

"You'd better wait outside, Slim," Ferry said. "I'll handle things here."

Surprise crossed Slim's face. "That's a pretty big order."

"I can take care of it."

Slim backed reluctantly to the door, keeping his eyes and his gun on the Leightons.

"I'm not going far," he said. "Try just one funny move and I'll be back—quick." He turned to Ferry. "All right, Ferry; it's your show now." He stepped through the door into the dark.

For an instant after Slim left, there wasn't a sound in the room.

"Unbuckle your gun belts and drop them on the floor," Ferry ordered. "One at a time, with your left hands. Start with Judd."

Judd choked with rage, his face purple. "I'll see you in—"

Ferry eared back the hammer on his gun. "Drop it!"

For a moment Ferry thought Judd was going to call his hand. With his brothers and hired gun hands behind him, they could easily cut Ferry down. But Judd knew as well as the others that Ferry would get him. Even a tenderfoot couldn't miss at that distance. All he had to do was squeeze the trigger.

His neck bulging in helpless fury, Judd slowly untied his holster and unbuckled his gun belt, letting it thump to the floor. One by one, belts hit the floor until all the Leighton men stood unarmed. Ferry motioned with his gun toward the opposite wall.

"Line up over there." He tried to keep his voice steady, hoping to hide his relief. But he wasn't safe yet. He wouldn't be safe until he was out of this building and far enough away so that the Leightons couldn't catch him.

The unarmed men moved slowly back to the wall. Ferry let his eyes slide over them until they rested on the light-haired Leighton brother.

"You're Joe Leighton, aren't you?"

"What of it?" came the sullen reply.

"I've got a job for you."

"I'm not looking for jobs from you."

Ferry relaxed a little. "You might like this one. I brought Miss Bradden here tonight. I'm afraid I won't have time to see her home properly. Would you do it for me?"

The frown left Joe's face. "Sure, I'll do that."

Ferry started backing toward the door. At least he had stopped one Leighton from joining the chase that would start the moment they were free to scoop up their guns and run for their horses. Ferry was sure Joe would think the job he had been given too important to neglect just to ride around the country trying to catch Dan Ferry.

As Ferry drew even with the women, he glanced over at Connie. "Sorry, Connie," he said. "I just didn't have much choice."

"I understand," she said. Ferry saw in her face that she didn't resent the arrangement he had made for her.

As Ferry reached the door, Judd bellowed a threat at him. "I'll get you if it's the last thing I ever do!"

Then Ferry was through the door and into the dimly lighted street. Bedlam broke out inside the hall. Ferry knew the Leightons were scrambling for their guns.

"Over here!" Slim called from the hitchrack where he was mounted and holding the reins of Ferry's horse.

"We've got to burn the breeze. This street will be full of lead in about a minute."

Ferry threw himself into the saddle. He knew Slim was right. Pursuit would be swift and it would be deadly.

V

The street was virtually deserted as Ferry and Slim kicked their horses into a gallop. There was a light in the lobby of the hotel, and lights were blazing in the Silver Spur saloon. But there were only three horses tied to the hitchrack in front of the saloon. Everybody was up the street at the town hall, where they had anticipated an exciting evening. Some were probably satisfied; others would feel cheated because guns hadn't blazed inside the hall.

As Ferry and Slim thundered past the saloon, the first gunshot from the town hall shattered the night, and Ferry bent lower over his saddle.

"They can't hit us this far away in the dark," Slim called gaily to Ferry. "Nobody's that good a shot."

"They might get lucky," Ferry flung back.

"If you're worried, better make that bronc think he's an eagle," Slim said. "I don't figure they like us much back there."

At the end of the street, the road swung to the west, aiming up the valley on the south side of Thunder Ridge. The sounds of fury and confusion back at the town hall dropped behind them. But Ferry knew that the fury would soon revive in a thunder of hoofbeats as the Leightons found their horses and took up the pursuit.

"Great way to break up a fight," Slim said, "using yourself for a target."

"Nobody was killed," Ferry shot back.

"Yet," Slim added. "Here they come!"

Ferry heard it, too: a rumble of hoofbeats thundering down the street. But Ferry and Slim had a good lead. Unless the Leightons had fast horses, it would be some time before they could get within six-gun range.

"Heading straight for the ranch?" Ferry asked.

"Can you think of a better place?" Slim asked. "Steve and the boys are there. They'd like nothing better than for us to bring the Leightons right to them."

As the pursuit pounded out of town behind them,

Ferry realized that he and Slim didn't have as big a lead as he had at first thought. The Leightons had made fast time getting mounted and on the trail.

Bending low over his saddle, Ferry urged his horse to the limit. He had no illusions about what would happen to him and Slim if the Leightons should catch up with them. Judd Leighton had been made to look ridiculous in front of practically everybody in the country when Ferry had forced him to take off his gun belt. If what Ferry had heard about him was right, Judd would consider that a stain on his reputation that would disgrace him until he blotted it out. And the only way he could blot it out was to erase the cause, Dan Ferry.

The trail paralleled the fringe of trees reaching down from Thunder Ridge. The dark shelter of those trees looked inviting to Ferry.

"Could we duck into these trees?" he called to Slim.

"We'd be trapped the minute we did," Slim said. "Look behind. See them? They can see us, too. The instant our horses vanished, they'd know where we'd gone."

Ferry acknowledged the wisdom of Slim's observation. But, unless Ferry was imagining it, those horses behind them were covering ground faster than he and Slim were. The ranch was still a long way ahead.

"They must have race horses," Ferry said.

"They've set fire to their tails, all right," Slim agreed.

Sporadic shooting started, but Slim and Ferry dropped off a ridge without being hit. Then Ferry saw Slim's plan. He pulled his horse into the edge of some trees. The swell of ground behind shut them off from view of the Leightons.

"Loop your reins over the saddle horn," Slim said hurriedly. "Get off and slap your horse over the rump. My horse will go on home. Your will follow him."

Ferry threw himself out of the saddle and whacked his horse over the hips. Slim did the same. The horses galloped back into the trail and on toward the ranch.

"Won't they see those horses don't have riders?" Ferry asked.

"Not till they're well past here, I hope," Slim said. "By then we won't be here, either. They could hunt all night and never find us in these trees. Come on."

Ferry nodded and followed Slim deeper into the trees that climbed the side of Thunder Ridge. Slim was completely confident of his ability to outwit the

Leightons, and Ferry, unfamiliar with his surroundings, had to put his faith in that confidence.

"Let's see what they do," Slim said, stopping.

Ferry would have preferred to move on to a safer distance from the road. But he said nothing and crouched with Slim as the Leightons came thundering over the ridge.

They swept past the spot where Ferry and Slim were crouching, and their guns opened up again.

"At least they're hitting their target now." Slim chuckled. "They're shooting at nothing, and they're bound to hit it."

"How long will it be before they find out they're chasing empty saddles?" Ferry asked.

"I doubt if they'll figure it out before they get to the ranch," Slim said. "Boy, I wish I could be there when they chase those horses into the Triangle F yard."

Ferry stood up. "At least walking isn't going to be as crowded here as the traffic was on that road a little while ago."

Occasional shots ripped the night as the Leightons rode on toward the Triangle F. Then suddenly a thunderous burst of firing rolled down the valley.

"They got there," Slim said with satisfaction. "Remind me to make sure Steve thanks me for bringing the Leightons to him."

The shooting lasted only a few minutes; then all was quiet. Ferry and Slim began moving through the trees.

"How far is it?" Ferry asked.

"A mile maybe," Slim said. "Let's get out in the road where the walking will be easier."

"Won't we have company there as the Leightons come back?"

Slim shook his head. "They won't come back this way. They'll go over the ridge to the Hooked J."

Ferry understood. He had come down that trail from the top of Thunder Ridge just that afternoon. It would be only a short ride from the Triangle F to Leighton's Hooked J by taking the trail over Thunder Ridge.

Still Ferry kept his ears open for the sound of horses as he and Slim made their way toward the ranch. But no sound came to break the quiet of the night.

"Better walk light if you want to get any sleep tonight," Slim said as he and Ferry crossed the yard toward the house and bunkhouse. Only an alley ten feet wide separated the two buildings.

"The boys light sleepers?" Ferry asked.

"Steve is when he's mad. And believe me, he's mad tonight. I don't want to have to go to the creek for a bucket of water to cool him off."

Slim went into the bunkhouse quietly, and Ferry opened the door of the big house and entered, crossing to the room Slim had indicated this afternoon would be his bedroom. Ferry was tired. It had been a busy day, but he wasn't sure it had been a successful one.

The sun was just tipping the eastern horizon, and Wong Ling had breakfast on the table, when Ferry came into the big dining room the next morning.

"Morning, boss," Slim greeted him cheerily. "Better watch Steve this morning. He's liable to bite you instead of his biscuit."

"I suppose you think I butted in where I wasn't wanted last night," Ferry said, pulling up a chair.

"I sure do," Steve Hayes said sullenly.

"He was all set to go to his own funeral last night," Slim said. "He didn't like it because you postponed it."

"I was taking care of myself," Hayes shot back

angrily.

Slim's face sobered. "The way I saw it, Steve, you didn't have the chance of a bogged-down steer. Judd's fast, and he got the jump on you with his draw. If Dan hadn't butted in when he did, you'd have been colder now than Golly Gee's day-old coffee."

"Wong Ling's coffee fresh and hot," the Chinese cook interrupted angrily.

Hayes ignored both Slim and the cook and turned his baleful glare on Ferry. "Well, you've had your look at the Leightons. Do you still think you can honey-talk them out of fighting?"

Ferry buttered the biscuit in his hand before answering. The Triangle F foreman had a strong point. But Ferry had a mine to locate. That would be a big enough job without a range war on his hands.

"I still think it's worth a try."

"Maybe you think you can wave a magic wand and tame every gun fighter along the ridge."

"He sure tamed the Leightons last night," Slim said.

"They weren't very tame when they rode in here," Lige Conklin, one of the crew, said.

"The boss dehorned them once," Slim said. "Made them shuck their hardware in the dance hall. Surely you should have been able to handle them when they got here."

"We handled them all right," Corky Wills, another hand, said with a grin. "If you'd let us know you were sending them out, we'd have been ready and we'd have kept them here, permanently."

Wong Ling charged in the door, carrying a dishpan which he'd had hanging on the outside of the house overnight. A hole had been drilled through the bottom by a bullet.

"Golly gee!" he exploded. "Keep Leighton men away from Wong Ling's pans!"

"Why don't you get a gun and keep them away yourself?" Slim suggested.

"Wong Ling cook, not fight. Wong Ling find ranch where they don't shoot holes in pans."

"I'll fix your pan," Slim said. "Guess nobody here was in much danger last night. That pan was ten feet from the door."

"If you made Judd Leighton shed his hardware last night, boss," Lige Conklin said, "you'd better ride with one hand on your gun now. Judd will be after your hide. And he'll get it, too, if you give him half a chance."

"How well can you shoot a gun, Dan?" Slim asked.

"Well enough," Ferry said.

"Not well enough to tangle with the Leightons, I'll bet," Hayes said disgustedly.

"Steve may be right," Slim said. "Come on out. Let's see what you can do."

Breakfast over, the men filed out into the yard. Ferry looked them over. Five rough and ready men. Ferry was still wearing his new clothes, and apparently he still looked like a tenderfoot to them.

"What do you want me to shoot at?" he asked.

"How about the corner post of the corral?" Slim said. "Come on down here."

Ferry moved over to the spot where Slim was waiting, only a few yards from the heavy corner post of the corral.

"How about that knot on the post?" Ferry asked.

"You can't hit that knot one time in ten," Hayes said quickly. "I'll bet you can't even hit the post."

"Just what will you bet?" Ferry said, anger bubbling up in him.

"I'll bet you the best horse I've got against a double eagle that you can't hit that knot two times out of three," Steve said, grinning condescendingly.

"Jupiter is his best horse, Dan," Slim said. "If you think you've got any chance of hitting that knot, he's worth risking twenty bucks on."

"It's a bet," Ferry said.

He lifted his gun and aimed carefully. Then he fired three times, allowing time only to correct his aim after the recoil following each shot. When he lowered the gun, Slim led the way to the post on a trot. The other men followed.

"Jumping jack rabbits!" Slim exclaimed. "Two dead center and the other one right in the edge of the knot. Looks like you've lost a horse, Steve."

Steve Hayes swore and crowded close to examine the post. Then he turned and stalked furiously toward the bunkhouse.

"Where did you learn to shoot like that?" Slim demanded.

"At college," Ferry said. "I belonged to the pistol team. And I've done plenty of shooting the last couple of years, too."

"Is your draw as good as your shooting?"

Ferry shook his head. "Afraid not. I'm no gun fighter."

"You'll have to be to last long around here," Slim

said. "Tell you what. You can already outshoot anybody on this range. I'll give you some lessons on getting your gun clear of leather. Then you can stand up to anything the Leightons can throw at you."

"I didn't come here to make a reputation as a gun fighter," Ferry said hesitantly. "I've got my reasons for stopping this fight as soon as possible."

"The fastest way to stop things sometimes is to finish them," Slim said. "It's the only way you'll stop this fight. Get plenty of ammunition and we'll go up in the edge of the trees and work on your draw."

Slim headed for the corral to saddle a couple of horses.

VI

Dan Ferry realized that his fight with the Leightons was only one part of his battle to take control of the Triangle F Ranch. With every passing hour, Steve Hayes, the foreman, was making it clearer that he had no respect for his new boss or the orders that he gave.

Ferry asked Slim about Hayes at the end of one of the lessons with the .45 that Slim insisted on giving Ferry.

"Is Hayes liable to take things in his own hands when he feels like it?"

Slim shrugged. "I'd say the odds are that he will. Until you can handle that gun a little better, he's not apt to consider you worth listening to."

"Maybe I'll have to teach him better," Ferry said.

"You can't fire him. He knows that. What else can

you do?"

"Show him who's boss, I reckon," Ferry said.

Slim grinned. "That makes sense. But just how do you figure on doing that? You own the ranch, but you don't own Steve Hayes."

"That's a piece of property I don't care to own," Ferry said. "But I've still got a notion I can put a stop to this fighting between the Triangle F and the Leightons. I'll never do it while Hayes keeps prodding the Leightons."

Slim stuffed the remainder of a box of ammunition into his saddle bag. "You've got that figured, all right. But just telling Steve what to do isn't going to make him do it."

"He respects force and that's all. Right?"

"You've dabbed your rope on the right critter now."

"If I made him and the rest of you boys stay home from the Fourth of July celebrations next Saturday, he'd change his thinking, wouldn't he?"

Slim whistled softly. "The whole country would change its thinking if you kept the Triangle F away from the celebration. That figures to be the battle of the century."

Ferry nodded. "That's what I gather from the talk

of the men. This battle is one I'd like to pass up. So—
the Triangle F crew will not go to Sundown next
Saturday."

Slim scratched his head. "I've gone along with you,
Dan, on everything you've done so far. But if you
make that an order, you'll have every man in the crew
to gun down to make it stick."

"There won't be any guns involved. You don't have
to back me if you don't want to. Just don't join them."

"Well," Slim said slowly, "I'll keep my fingers
crossed. But I can't say that I'll be hoping you win.
That scrap at the celebration Saturday is one I'm not
figuring on missing."

The ride to the house was a silent one.

Ferry and Slim dismounted at the corral and loos-
ened the cinches on their saddles, then headed for the
house where the crew was lounging on the veranda.

"I hope you know what you're doing, Dan," Slim
said. "Nobody pushes Steve around."

Ferry made no reply but strode on toward the
house, Slim tagging along behind as though reluctant
to witness what was about to happen.

"Ready to take on Billy the Kid now?" Hayes asked
with a condescending grin.

Ferry shook his head, matching the foreman's grin. "I expect to take on my foreman if he doesn't obey orders."

The grin slid off Hayes' face. "Just what order are you talking about?"

"The Triangle F crew is going to stay home Saturday."

For a moment there wasn't a sound on the veranda. If one of the men had dropped dead in his tracks, it wouldn't have created a more stunned silence.

"We're going to that celebration," Hayes said finally in slow distinct tones. "And no pin-eared dude is going to stop us."

"I'm going to stop you," Ferry said quietly. "I've given my orders. You're staying home."

Steve Hayes got up, the muscles in his neck and shoulders working. "We'll see who's the boss here, if that's the way you want it."

Ferry nodded. "That's the way I want it."

Deliberately Ferry unbuckled his gun belt and tossed it on the veranda. Hayes watched him; then, with a satisfied grin, he did the same.

"If you want it slow and painful, that's how you'll get it," he said, and stepped down into the yard.

"Is it agreed that the winner bosses this outfit?" Ferry asked.

Hayes merely grunted and nodded, the eagerness in his eyes giving them a brilliance that reminded Ferry of a cat about to spring on a mouse.

The rest of the crew formed a loose circle around the two men in the yard as they slowly circled each other. Out of the corner of his eye, Ferry saw Slim watching intently, his head shaking slowly.

Ferry didn't underestimate his opponent. Steve Hayes was about the same height as Ferry, but he was nearly twenty pounds heavier. And much of that weight was in his massive shoulders and arms. Ferry knew that Hayes was a powerful man and would rather die than lose this fight.

Hayes dropped into a crouch, arms wide, feet shuffling. Then he drove forward like a mad bull. Ferry sidestepped and landed a stinging blow on the foreman's nose as he went past.

Hayes roared in anger and wheeled to drive in again. It took all the skill Ferry had learned in two years of boxing at college to keep out of Hayes' way. As he evaded each charge, Ferry landed one or two sharp blows. But they seemed to have no effect whatsoever on Hayes except to heighten his rage. The foreman's capacity to absorb punishment amazed Ferry.

Hayes came in again and again, arms swinging wildly. And not all those blows were missing their marks. One caught Ferry in the side and made him gasp for breath, while another broke through his guard and clipped him on the ear, causing the house and yard to reel drunkenly before his eyes for a moment.

The terrific pace began to tell on Ferry as he feinted and dodged to avoid the foreman's blows, pounding punishment into the man on every charge. Still Hayes came on relentlessly. Ferry began to doubt that he could outlast the husky foreman.

Then, when Ferry was wondering if he'd have to quit, he became aware that the foreman's charges were tapering off in speed and ferocity. Slowly the realization that he had found a man he couldn't bull over was beginning to seep into Hayes' mind.

Ferry bided his time, conserving what strength he had left. Hayes drove forward again, not willing to give up and knowing no other way to keep fighting. But his arms were swinging wearily and his breath was labored.

Ferry chose that moment to launch an attack of his own. Surprise as much as weariness caught Hayes off guard. Ferry's first blow landed flush on the bruised nose, and Hayes dropped back, roaring like a wounded elephant. Ferry followed up with a smash on the foreman's chin. Hayes staggered back until the side of the house caught and held him.

Ferry was ready to quit, but Hayes pushed himself away from the house and came at Ferry again.

Ferry stood his ground and put what strength he had left in two hard blows that landed squarely on the point of the foreman's chin. Hayes's face twisted to one side; then, with a heavy sigh, he collapsed in a heap.

Ferry reeled to the veranda and dropped down on the steps. Dimly he watched Slim move over and bend over Hayes.

"I'll be a ring-tailed monkey!" Slim muttered. "I didn't think I'd ever see the day."

Ferry wasn't sure how long he sat there, trying desperately to catch his breath and get his befuddled thoughts straightened out. He couldn't let the crew know how near complete exhaustion he was.

Finally Steve Hayes began to move. He sat up and

shook his head a few times like a stunned steer. Then a dull gleam of fury replaced the vacant stare in his eyes. He reeled to his feet and started toward the porch.

"Let me get my gun!" he muttered thickly. "I'll show you how to fight like a man."

Head down, he stumbled to the veranda. But there he stopped, staring at the feet blocking his path. Slowly his head lifted until he was staring into Slim's cold eyes.

"Get out of my way!" Hayes shouted hoarsely. "I'm going to kill him."

Slim didn't move. "You agreed that the winner would be boss," he said, his voice velvety soft. "You lost a fair fight. Dan is boss now." He stepped aside. "If you're not man enough to take a licking, then go on and get your gun. But if you do, I'll kill you the second you touch it."

Slim's voice was still soft, with no trace of emotion, but there was no mistaking the deadly sting in it. It penetrated the red fog clouding Hayes' brain. All the anger and strength seemed to melt out of the foreman's legs, and he sank down on the edge of the veranda, his face ashen.

"All right," he whispered. "Ferry is boss."

Ferry pushed himself up from the veranda steps and moved over to his foreman, holding out his hand. "No hard feelings?"

Hayes ignored Ferry's hand. "You're boss. You give the orders; we'll follow them."

Ferry's eyes hardened. "That's fine with me. Don't forget it."

"No celebration, boss?" Lige Conklin ventured cautiously.

Ferry looked at the disappointed men standing around him. His order to stay away from the celebration had served its purpose. "Maybe we'll go. It all depends on the sheriff in town."

Swift grins spread over the faces around Ferry. Slim's grin was the widest of all.

"That sounds more like it. But what's the sheriff got to do with it?"

"Can't tell you till I see him," Ferry said. "Want to ride into town with me, Slim?"

"Sure. But if you're looking for help from Sid Belcher, you'd have more luck looking for a daisy under a slimy rock."

"I take it you have no love for the sheriff."

"You've got the picture. Let's put on the feed bag before we go to town, Dan. You need an hour stretched out on a bunk before you ride anywhere, anyway."

Ferry knew that Slim was right, but he wasn't going to let the rest of the crew, particularly Steve Hayes, know that he was almost too exhausted to mount a horse.

"All right," he agreed. "We'll wait until after dinner. Tell Wong Ling not to be too long with the grub."

Ferry felt much better after an hour's wait for dinner. When he and Slim left the yard to ride to town, a few bruises and aching muscles were the only reminders he had of his fight with Hayes.

"What do you have against Sheriff Belcher?" Ferry asked as they neared Sundown.

Slim shrugged. "He's just a poor stick of a sheriff, that's all. All bark and no bite."

"Harmless, is he?"

"That's according," Slim countered. "If he's got a grudge against you, don't turn your back to him."

"Well, he has no grudge against me," Ferry said.

"I reckon you figure he can stop this fighting," Slim said as they rode into the dusty street. "But you're wrong, Dan. He couldn't if he wanted to. And I don't reckon he wants to."

"He represents the law here," Ferry said, and reined Jupiter toward the hitchrack in front of the little building that had "Sheriff's Office" printed in uneven letters across the front.

Ferry led the way inside the building. A short, heavy-set, almost fat man sat at a spur-scarred desk, hat pulled over his eyes, half asleep. He grunted when he heard the thump of boots on his floor, pushed his hat back and stared at his visitors from bloodshot eyes.

"What do you want?" he demanded sleepily, wiping the slobbers from his chin.

Ferry tried to hide his disgust at the sight of the sheriff. "I'm Dan Ferry. I guess you know Slim Walters."

The sheriff nodded. "Well enough."

"It's your job to keep law and order here, isn't it?"

"Sure." The last shred of sleep vanished from Sheriff Sid Belcher's eyes, and he looked at Ferry suspiciously. "What about it?"

"What are you planning to do about the celebration Saturday?"

Belcher looked puzzled. "What am I supposed to do? Wave a flag all day?"

"You know what I mean," Ferry said, his patience wearing thin. "There'll be trouble that day and you know it. How many deputies will you have on duty?"

"Deputies? I won't have any. I never need deputies."

Ferry's eyes bored into the sheriff. "You're going to need an army of deputies that day to keep order."

The sheriff drummed his fingers on his desk. "Maybe so. But if I keep things too quiet, a lot of people are going to be disappointed. They're expecting a big day."

"You don't want a battle right in your streets, do you?"

"Of course not," Belcher said hastily. "I'll do my best to keep the peace."

"It's going to be as peaceful as a prayer meeting Saturday," Slim said mockingly from the doorway. "Come on, Dan. We're wasting our time here."

Ferry ignored Slim. "I've got a proposition to make, Sheriff," he said. "I'll vouch for the good behavior of my men if you can get the Leightons to promise the same for their outfit."

Belcher's eyes popped. "You mean call off the fight?"

Ferry slammed a fist on the desk. "It's a celebration Saturday; not a fight! How about it?"

"Sure, sure," Belcher said, rubbing his chin. "Do you think you can keep your boys in line?"

"I can," Ferry said. "How about the Leightons?"

"The Leightons are a hard bunch to deal with," Belcher said slowly. "But I'll see what I can do."

VII

Rosanne Leighton reined up at the north end of the main street of Sundown and waited until the two riders going the other way were out of sight. She didn't want Dan Ferry or Slim Walters to see her. When they were gone, she nudged her horse into motion again, wondering what they had been doing in town.

As she rode down the street and reined in at the hitchrack in front of Hartlett's Grocery, she saw Sheriff Sid Belcher lounging in the doorway of his office directly across from the store. There was a thoughtful frown on his face.

Rosanne had two errands to take care of in town, and she dispatched the first one quickly, buying the things on the list she and her mother had made out. Then, with her groceries tucked into her saddle bags, she moved down to the café which was next door to the store.

The café was empty when Rosanne entered, and that was to her liking. She wanted to talk to Connie Bradden, and she didn't need an audience. A minute after the door closed behind Rosanne, Connie came from the kitchen.

"Oh, I thought it was Mamie," Connie said. "She always comes over about this time of day for a cup of black coffee."

"Aren't you about due for a vacation from here?" Rosanne asked.

Connie smiled. "Due maybe, but I'm not liable to get one. And I can't afford to quit."

"I thought maybe you could come out and stay with me for a few days. I get lonesome for company out there."

"With four brothers?" Connie exclaimed. "I wouldn't call that lonesome."

"That's just it. All brothers and no sisters. And they're so wrapped up in this fight with the Triangle F, they're not decent company."

Connie nodded. "I see what you mean. When would you want me to come out?"

"Whenever Mr. Snelly will let you off," Rosanne said.

"I'll see what he says," Connie said, and moved quickly toward the back of the building.

Rosanne sat on one of the stools in front of the counter. She and Connie had been friends almost from the time Connie had come there. Connie had been out at the Hooked J several times, but not recently.

Connie came back into the main room, her glowing face telling its own story.

"He says I can have three days off right after the Fourth. There won't be much business then, anyway."

"Good." Roseanne slid off the stool. "I'll ride in Sunday morning and we'll go out together."

When she rode into the Hooked J yard, Rosanne saw that the Leightons had company. A short, rather pudgy man with reddish hair was talking earnestly to Judd just a short distance from the gate. Rosanne kept her eyes on the visitor as she dismounted and started to unsaddle her horse.

Joe Leighton, the youngest of her brothers and Rosanne's favorite, came out of the barn and took over the task of unsaddling the horse.

"Who is the stranger?" Rosanne asked.

"Fellow named Link Dalton. Don't you know him?"

Rosanne nodded. "A little. I never liked him. What is he doing here?"

"Got business with Judd."

"What kind of business could he have?" Rosanne asked suspiciously.

"I'm not sure. He said something about a deal."

"He's been in the country before, hasn't he, Joe?"

Joe nodded. "Sure. He says he used to ride for Ad Ferry."

"Then what's he doing here now?" Rosanne demanded. "We don't need any of Ferry's men on the Hooked J."

"He says he knows something important. He wants to make a deal with us for that information."

"I don't trust him," Rosanne said as she headed for the house.

She passed close to Link Dalton and Judd on her way to the house, and Dalton grinned at her, his yellow-green eyes sweeping over her possessively.

"Maybe I ought to do my business with your sister," Dalton said. "I'll bet she'd listen to my ideas."

Judd scowled darkly. "You leave her out of this. Go on in the house, Rosanne."

Rosanne obeyed without a word of protest and went to her room to wait for Joe.

She finally heard his familiar tread on the porch. When Joe came into the living room, she opened her door and motioned him into her room. He came a little reluctantly."

"You don't like Dalton's deal, do you?" Rosanne said after studying his face for a moment.

"I sure don't," he blurted. "He's as crooked as a dog's hind leg."

"What does he want?"

"That's just it," Joe said. "He didn't ask Judd to do much that we wouldn't do, anyway. And he promised to show Judd how to get to Secret Valley where old Ad Ferry's mine is."

"How does he know about that?"

"He says he trailed old Ad up there one day when he was working for him," Joe said. "Judd jumped at that bait like a starved trout. But Dalton isn't one to hand over information like that without getting something in return."

"What do you think he wants, Joe?"

"The only thing I can figure is Dan Ferry. He mentioned he'd like to capture Ferry alive. I think he's afraid to tackle that job alone. So he's willing to show us where Secret Valley is to get our help in capturing Ferry."

"That could be," Rosanne said. "Is that what he asked Judd?"

"Not exactly. He asked Judd to clean out the Triangle F Ranch right away and capture Dan Ferry; then he'd show Judd where the valley is. Now he knows we're going to settle things with the Triangle F as soon as we can. Dalton isn't putting all his cards on the table."

"Maybe Dalton can't find the mine, even though he does know where Secret Valley is," Rosanne said. "Maybe he thinks he can torture the information out of Dan Ferry if he can capture him."

Joe's face brightened. "That's it, Sis! It's got to be! And once he gets hold of Ferry and finds out where the mine is, he'll forget that he made any deal with Judd."

"Is Judd going along with Dalton's deal?"

"Sure. We'll wind up doing the dirty job catching Dan Ferry, and Link Dalton will get the mine and all the gold in it."

"Link Dalton isn't going to stay around the ranch,

is he?" Rosanne asked.

"Talks like it. I don't like that, either."

Rosanne frowned. "I don't, either. I don't like the way he looks at me, like a weasel."

"If he ever lays a finger on you, Rosanne, let me know," Joe said fiercely. "I'll kill him!"

VIII

It was Friday when Sheriff Sid Belcher rode into
the Triangle F yard with the news that the Leightons
had agreed to the truce for the celebration the next day.

Dan Ferry looked over his men, who had poured out
of the house where they had just finished dinner. Suspicion was on every face.

"Did Judd Leighton tie any strings to that?" Ferry
asked.

The sheriff shook his head. "Nope. He was mad as
a rain-soaked hornet at first, but he finally agreed. No
trouble from anybody. Me and my deputies will jail
anybody who starts a fuss."

"I don't like the sound of it," Slim said flatly. "That
doesn't sound like Judd Leighton."

"Judd gave me his word," Belcher said. "There

won't be any trouble tomorrow unless you boys start it."

The sheriff wheeled his horse and pounded out of the yard in a cloud of dust.

"There's a trick to it somewhere," Steve Hayes grunted darkly. "Judd Leighton wouldn't agree to take a million dollar gift if a Ferry was involved."

"He has agreed not to start trouble tomorrow," Ferry said. "We've agreed to the same thing. If anybody breaks that agreement, it won't be us."

He turned on his heel and marched back into the house.

Ferry led his men into Sundown the next morning. The town was filling rapidly. Excitement was an undercurrent racing through the town.

It seemed to Ferry that every man, woman and child within a radius of fifty miles must be there. The only ones missing were the Leightons. And that caused Ferry more worry than if they had been in the crowd milling up and down the street.

"Where do you figure they are?" Slim asked Ferry as they moved through the crowd jamming the sidewalks.

"I wish I knew," Ferry said.

"They'll show," Slim said positively.

Ferry nodded. "I'd feel better if they were here right now."

"I know what you mean, Dan." Slim looked carefully up and down the street. "I'll see you later."

Ferry expected Slim to head for the Silver Spur Saloon, but he went in the other direction, turning into Kitter's Hardware Store.

On every hand as Ferry moved through the crowd he heard speculation as to the time Judd Leighton would lead his men into town.

Ferry could feel the tension building. It couldn't go on this way much longer without something snapping.

When it did snap, it wasn't where Ferry expected it at all. The crowd in front of the saloon suddenly began buzzing like an alerted rattler and parted reluctantly to let four men come through the swinging doors onto the board sidewalk.

Ferry hurried toward the spot when he saw two of Sheriff Belcher's special deputies prodding two Triangle F men, Lige Conklin and Pug Klepper, through the crowd.

"Call off these tinhorns," Conklin yelled when he

saw Ferry.

Ferry stepped in front of the four men, blocking their way. "What are the charges?" he asked.

"Disturbing the peace," one of the deputies growled.

"We weren't doing no such thing!" Conklin howled.

"Arguing with an officer of the law is disturbing the peace," one of the deputies said.

Ferry couldn't picture Pug Klepper arguing with anybody with words. In the week Ferry had been on the Triangle F, he hadn't heard Klepper speak half a dozen times.

Although he didn't like the looks of things, Ferry could see no way to change them right then, so he stepped aside. If he held up the deputies any longer, he would probably wind up in jail with Conklin and Klepper.

Ferry was still looking across the street toward the jail when another commotion turned him back toward the saloon. Another of Belcher's special deputies was coming through the door, Corky Wills riding the muzzle of his gun.

Suspicion glinted in Ferry's eyes as he stopped the deputy. "Same charges as the one against Conklin and Klepper?"

The deputy touched an eye tenderly where it was already beginning to turn red. "He didn't like it because his sidekicks were arrested."

Ferry stepped aside and let the deputy past, then followed him across the street to the jail, taking up a stand just outside the front window of the sheriff's office.

When the two deputies who had jailed Lige Conklin and Pug Klepper came striding across the street from the saloon with Steve Hayes in front of them, alarm gripped Ferry. Of the five-man crew who had ridden into Sundown with him that morning, only Slim remained free.

"Your idea is working out dandy, isn't it?" Hayes snapped as he passed Ferry.

Ferry didn't make any reply. Anything he did now would mean risking an open fight with the deputies. And it had been his idea to keep everything peaceful.

He glanced at Belcher. The sheriff was marching complacently back and forth over a short section of boardwalk in front of his office, completely ignoring his deputies. Slim was still in the doorway of Cy Kitter's store, but he was no longer leaning idly against the jamb. He was standing at a careless alert, a position that Ferry had already learned to recognize. Probably Slim was next on the deputies' list to arrest. Ferry knew they'd have their hands full when they tried it.

The deputies gathered in a knot in front of the Silver Spur, and Ferry guessed they were discussing ways to take Slim without a fight. But before they could move away from the saloon, a clatter of hoofbeats at the north end of the street arrested all activity and turned every eye in that direction. All sound except that of the approaching riders died. The highlight of the day had come; the Leightons had arrived.

Ferry watched the riders swing into the street and rein up dramatically. Almost without a sound, the street emptied, leaving only the sheriff standing a few feet from the corner of the jail. Ferry faded back into the doorway of the jail. He looked down at Kitter's. Slim had disappeared, too.

The Leightons dismounted in front of the livery stable at the end of the street and tied their horses. Then they formed a line across the street and began a slow deliberate march toward the jail.

Ferry recognized Judd just half a step ahead of the others. The twins, Jule and Jake, and Joe were to Judd's right, while three other men flanked Judd on the left. Ferry remembered seeing those three men at the dance the other night. Apparently they were on the Hooked J payroll. Ferry looked in vain for the stocky figure of Link Dalton. Somehow he had half expected him to be riding with the Leightons today. But the redhead wasn't there.

Sheriff Sid Belcher retreated to the front of the jail, nervously fingering the star on his vest. Fifty feet from the jail, Judd held up his hand and the row of men halted.

"I want those men you've got in jail, Belcher," Judd demanded.

Hot prickles of rage swept over Ferry. He had suspected this whole set-up was a trap when the first Triangle F men had been arrested that morning. Now he had the positive proof.

Ferry looked at Belcher, who had backed against the wall. "You can't have them," the sheriff said. "They're under the protection of the law."

Judd started another slow advance. "I don't care about your law. I want those men."

"Now take it easy, Judd," Belcher whined.

Judd hesitated, his hand close to his gun. "Well, are you going to fight or get out of the way?"

The sheriff shifted uneasily from one foot to the other. "I don't have much chance to fight."

"That's a fact," Judd said. "Get out of the way." He led his men forward.

Ferry shot a glance down the street. The deputies, who had been so conspicuous a few minutes before, were nowhere in sight now. Blind rage gripped him. He had been suckered into a trap he'd set up himself. He leaped out of the doorway, his gun leveled at Judd's broad chest.

"That's far enough!" The words hit like hailstones on a tin roof.

Every movement on the street stopped as if time had suspended all life for an instant. Ferry realized that Judd Leighton had been concentrating on Belcher and hadn't been aware of Ferry's presence in the jail doorway.

Judd's hand streaked for his gun. But even before Ferry could react, a voice cut through the air like a whip.

"I wouldn't do that, Judd!"

Judd's hand froze again an inch from the butt of his gun. He turned slowly, the rest of the men following his lead.

Slim stood on the porch of Kitter's store, his gun covering the seven men in the street. A wide grin spread across his face, and his voice was soft and almost cheerful.

"Why don't you go ahead and draw, Judd? You've got six men with you. You can cut me down. Of course I'll take you and a couple more with me." The grin faded then, and his voice took on the edge of a cutlass. "Either fill your hands or lift them!"

Slowly Judd raised his hands; the other six men in the street followed his example.

Ferry stepped up to the sheriff. "I'll take that gun of yours, Belcher. It doesn't seem to be of any use to you." He lifted the gun from its holster. "Now get in there and unlock those cells."

"Wait a minute, Ferry," the sheriff blustered. "You're breaking the law."

Ferry jammed his gun deep into Belcher's side. "If my name was Leighton, it would be all right, wouldn't it? Get in there!"

Belcher grunted, his eyes popping in fear. He spun around and shuffled rapidly inside, fumbling with the keys.

Ferry followed to the door. There he stopped, his

gun still centered on the sheriff. He glanced back at the street. The Leightons were beginning to fidget; Slim wouldn't be able to hold them quiet much longer. Belcher was still fumbling clumsily through his pile of keys.

Ferry stepped inside and jabbed the gun into Belcher's ribs. "If you don't have one of those cells open in ten seconds, you'll leave this jail on a slab!"

Belcher lunged toward the first cell, the right key miraculously appearing in his hand. A minute later the last of the cell doors swung open.

"Get your guns, men," Ferry said. He pushed Belcher into the last cell and slammed the door. "You cool your heels in there."

A shot split the tension outside. Ferry whirled toward the door. Hayes and the rest of the men were fishing their guns out of the sheriff's desk.

"Do we get to fight now?" Hayes asked with a sneer.

Ferry ignored the sarcasm. "Hurry it up. Slim can't handle them alone."

"If he is still alive," Lige Conklin said, finally getting his gun and running to the window.

To prove that Slim was very much alive, a volley of shots rolled out of the doorway of Cy Kitter's hard-

ware store. One of Leighton's hired hands running for
he shelter of Ed Harnett's Grocery sprawled in the
dust ten feet short of his goal.

Guns began pouring lead out of the jail window and
door. The big window of Harnett's Grocery was shattered, and broken glass showered the porch. Then, as
the Leightons found concealed positions inside the
store, bullets began to thud into the wall of the jail.

"Keep out of sight," Hayes warned. "Those fellows
can shoot."

Ferry didn't need the warning. But he snapped as
many shots across the street as any of the men around
him.

When his gun was empty, he dropped down on the
door to reload. It was then that he heard the groaning
of one of the men who had been at the window. Pug
Klepper stretched out on the floor a few feet from the
window, and Ferry moved over quickly to examine
him.

"Can't do nothing for him," Hayes said callously.
"But we'll even things for him before we're through."

Ferry turned back to his task of reloading his gun,
sick at the thought of what was going on.

He reached the door, ready to open fire again, when

a shout of triumph came from the window.

"That evens things for Pug!" Hayes said, his face burning with malicious joy.

"Which one did you get, Steve?" Conklin asked.

"Coalie Morton," Hayes reported. "Just winged him, I reckon. But he won't be fighting any more for a while. Nothing left over there now but the four Leightons and Otto Miller. Let's clean them out and be done with it."

The guns in the jail beat a rapid tattoo against the store front and the shelves and boxes inside. Slim's gun was still barking from the doorway of Kitter's.

It was some time before Ferry became aware that there were no answering shots coming from the store across the street. He stopped firing about the same time the rest of the men did. The deathly silence that hung over the town was more appalling than the firing had been.

"It's a trick," Lige Conklin said after a moment.

But a sudden commotion at the upper end of the street proved Conklin wrong.

"They're running out on us!" Hayes yelled, and dashed into the street, emptying his gun at the Leightons, now racing out of range.

A parting volley from the Leightons kicked up puffs
f dust around the Triangle F men as they poured into
he street. Slim leaped off the porch of Kitter's store.

"I guess we showed them how the cat licked his
ar," Slim said, his grin even wider than usual.
"Where's Pug?"

"Cashed in," Hayes said carelessly. "But I winged
Morton. And you got their other gun hand. How come
ou didn't take Judd?"

"I was aiming at him," Slim admitted. "But Walton
got in the way. They were harder to hit than a flock
f running turkeys."

"Who fired that first shot?" Ferry asked.

"I'm not sure," Slim said. "I think it was one of
hose peace-loving deputies. That sure was a honey of
a frame-up, Dan."

Ferry's eyes kindled. "I know." He turned to the
thers. "You'd better go home. I'll be along pretty
oon."

IX

When Ferry and Slim rode into the Triangle F yard, only one horse was standing at the hitchrack in front of the house.

"Wonder where Steve and Corky are," Slim said. "This is Lige's horse."

Ferry and Slim had started toward the house when Lige came out the door. He didn't wait for Ferry's question.

"Steve and Corky said they had some business to attend to." He held up a bandaged hand. "I got a little scratch in that fracas in town, and I thought I'd better come on and wash it up."

"What kind of business?" Ferry asked apprehensively.

Lige Conklin shrugged. "You'll have to ask them.

They didn't tell me their secrets."

It was an hour past noon when Slim announced from the doorway that Hayes and Corky Wills were coming.

"They're riding like Satan was on their tail," he said.

The two riders pulled to a halt in front of the house and swung down. They came inside, wide grins of satisfaction spreading over their faces.

"Who was prodding you?" Slim asked.

"Not sure anybody was after we topped the ridge," Hayes reported. "But we sure had plenty of trail hounds smelling our tracks on the other side."

"Who?"

Hayes snorted. "Who do you reckon?"

"Any special reason?" Ferry asked.

Corky Wills took up the explanation. "Plenty! We circled around ahead of the Leightons and hid in that patch of rocks close to Otto Miller's place." He turned to Ferry to explain. "Miller has a little spread all his own. He always rode with the Leightons, though."

"The Leightons were making mighty poor time," Hayes said, "because of Morton being hurt so bad. We waited till Miller turned off from the rest of the bunch and headed for his place. When he got to the rocks, we raised up and let him have it."

"Why did you pick Miller?" Slim asked.

"It was Steve's idea," Wills said. "And it was a good one. He was the only one that was going to get off by himself. We weren't about to tackle the whole bunch."

"Didn't the others hear the shooting?" Slim asked. "Those rocks aren't far off the main trail."

"Hear it?" Corky Wills exploded. "I'd hope to smile they heard it! They were on our trail in nothing flat. We really had to pound leather to get out of there."

"We got rid of one more of the Leighton outfit, anyway," Hayes said with satisfaction.

"Without giving him a chance," Ferry added.

Hayes whirled on him. "Are you going soft on us again? I thought you'd be ready to fight now."

"I am ready to fight," Ferry snapped, "but not to murder."

"They'd have murdered us without batting an eye if they'd gotten us out of jail today," Hayes said. "We just managed to do what they couldn't do."

"Are you forgetting, Steve, that it was Dan who kept

the Leightons from taking you out of jail?" Slim asked.

Hayes scowled at Ferry. "No. And I'm not forgetting how it happened we got in there in the first place, either."

"We're in this thing to the end now," Ferry said. "We'll fight the Leightons every chance we get, but we won't murder them from ambush. I want that understood."

"Old Ad was like that, too," Hayes said disgustedly. "Look what it got him. Hardly a decent funeral."

"Dan, you said you were going to fight this war the way Judd wanted to fight it," Slim said softly. "Don't expect him to wait till you're facing him before he shoots."

"Just because I'm fighting a skunk doesn't mean I have to smell like one," Ferry said.

"You will before the fight's over," Slim said.

"What do we do now?" Hayes asked, watching Ferry speculatively. "Sit back and wait for the Leightons to deal the cards again?"

"Let's go over the ridge and clean them out," Corky Wills said excitedly. "There's just the four Leighton boys and their old man now. And he's got a busted wing."

"You're forgetting Belcher and his deputies," Lige Conklin put in.

"They're in town," Wills said. "We can clean out the Leightons and be gone before they know anything about it."

Slim, usually the daredevil of the bunch, shook his head. "We might get more than we bargained for. If we'd been walloped in town like they were, what would we expect?"

"We'd look for them to come charging in here to finish us off," Hayes said.

"They'll expect the same," Ferry said, catching Slim's line of thought. "We'd probably be riding into a trap if we went over there. I'm going up on the ridge and take a look down there. I don't want anybody leaving here till I get back."

Slim went outside with Ferry. "Better be careful, Dan. That ridge is a good place to get killed if you're careless. It's a scouting post for the Leightons, too, you know."

Ferry nodded. "I know."

He didn't add that he was thinking it was where Ad had been killed, too. He wanted to look around up there. During the battle old Ad might have lost something that nobody had found.

The ridge was wrapped in the heavy silence of a midday calm when Ferry reined up at the big rock that stood like a sentinel watching over the two valleys.

He dismounted and led his horse into the trees and tied him. Bringing only his binoculars, he came back to the rock.

He leaned against the big rock and trained his binoculars on the trail leading out of the Leighton yard. The yard itself was obscured by the trees along the steep slope. Almost immediately he picked up a rider leaving the Hooked J. A moment's study showed him it was the storekeeper, Ed Hartlett. Hartlett hadn't wasted any time delivering the message Ferry had given him.

For quite a while Ferry let the glasses wander idly over the valley while his mind struggled with the problems facing him. Then the glasses dipped lower without conscious guiding until they centered on the trail leading up the ridge from the Hooked J.

He leaped back in surprise. In the magnified circle was a horse and rider. He jerked the glasses from his eyes and ducked behind the rock. Glancing back, he noted with relief that the rider, Rosanne Leighton, obviously hadn't seen him. She was studying the horn of her saddle, evidently having her own battle with problems.

Ferry stayed back out of sight, not sure just how he should meet this situation. After the battle in town this morning, anybody from the Triangle F would have to be out of his mind to trust a Leighton, even a girl.

The sound of a horse's hoof striking a rock, muffled by the warm heavy air, told Ferry that Rosanne had reached the other side of the big rock. Ferry's horse whinnied shrilly from the trees where he was tied. Ferry moved out to where he could see Rosanne facing the sound, her gun in her hand. In three noiseless strides, he reached her side.

"Not that way," he said softly. "Over here."

She snapped around, her gun spinning to cover him. But his hand shot out, pinning her hand to her side.

"Better let me take that. We'll have a more pleasant visit."

He slid the gun out of her hand and stuck it inside his belt while she glared at him like a cornered cougar.

"Take your hands off me!" she snapped.

"Whatever you say," he said, grinning as he stepped

back. "Would you mind getting off your horse?"

"I'm comfortable right here," she said icily.

"Maybe you are, but I'm not. You're too handy with that rifle."

She swung down angrily. "Now are you satisfied?"

"For the moment. What did Hartlett have to say?"

Her eyes flashed. "You ought to know. He was delivering your message. You're starting off great, too, killing Otto Miller from ambush."

His face went grim. "That wasn't done on my orders. I don't shoot from ambush."

"Your men do," Rosanne said acidly. "That's the same thing."

"Not quite," he said, fighting to control his anger. "I'm not exactly like the men who work for me. What other man down on the Triangle F would have taken your gun without throwing his own gun on you?"

Her black eyes bored into him. "Any other man from down there who tried it would have been dead by now."

"Am I to take that as a personal compliment because you haven't killed me?"

Color suddenly flooded her face. "Take it and go hang!" she said sharply, her fists clenched at her side.

He grinned, partly at her frustration and partly just because he felt like grinning. "I'll take the compliment and leave the hanging for some other time." He motioned to the binoculars swinging from her neck. "I suppose you came up here to do some spying. Go ahead. I'll watch your valley; you watch mine."

"If you see anything down there," she said acidly, "it will be something you won't want to see."

"Maybe," he agreed. "But I like to know when I'm going to be hit even if I can't get out of the way."

She took in a sharp breath and held it. Ferry turned quickly. Rosanne was looking down at the Triangle F buildings and uncasing her binoculars with precise movements.

Ferry stared down at the buildings, too. A rider was just leaving the corral on the trail toward town. Ferry lifted his glasses and focused them, bringing the rider into the magnified circle. It was Steve Hayes, his foreman.

"More of your orders?" Rosanne demanded sharply.

"His orders were to stay put till I got back," Ferry said, lowering his glasses.

"Doesn't look like your men obey very well," she said sarcastically.

"Guess I'll have to enforce some rules," he said, casing his binoculars.

"Maybe you can show them more clever ways to lay an ambush," she said.

Ferry didn't even turn back to make a reply.

X

When Wong Ling sounded the breakfast call the next morning, Steve Hayes hadn't returned to the Triangle F. Ferry had a cold lump of apprehension in his middle as he headed for the breakfast table. He saw the long faces around the table and noted the anxious glances shot at the door.

"The dance must have lasted late," Slim finally observed casually.

"Yeah," Lige Conklin agreed. "It must have been a real late one for Steve."

Breakfast was half over when a clatter of hoofbeats echoed in the yard. That ended the meal as effectively as if the food had all suddenly disappeared. Every chair scraped back and there was a concerted rush for the door.

Hugh Bradford was just dismounting from a lathered bay as the men, led by Slim and Ferry, poured onto the veranda.

"Know what happened to Steve?" Slim asked, voicing the question they all wanted to ask.

"Yeah." Bradford crossed the distance from the hitchrack to the veranda in long purposeful strides. "That's what I came over to tell you. Steve was killed last night."

"Killed?"

Hugh Bradford nodded. "He was knifed out behind the town hall."

"Did you see the fight?" Slim asked.

"Not sure there was much of a fight. I was at the dance, but I didn't see what happened to Steve."

"Do you know who killed him?" Corky Wills asked.

Bradford sat down on the veranda steps. "I can't prove it, but I know, all right."

"Who?"

"Judd Leighton. Who else?"

"So he went back to town," Ferry said.

"He was there, big as sin," Bradford said, then settled back, leaning against the post at the corner of the steps. "I got to the dance last night just in time to see Steve parade in with Mamie. Half an hour later Judd came. He was the only Leighton there, and he didn't act surprised to see Steve.

"It wasn't long till Steve and Judd locked horns over dancing with Mamie. She egged them on, too. Then, when it looked like a showdown was coming right there on the floor, she sent Judd away, telling him she was sticking with Steve."

"And he went?" Slim asked in amazement.

"Yeah," Bradford said. "Seemed funny to me, too. He threatened to get even with Steve, but that was all. Then he just walked off. I smelled a rat, but Steve didn't. He acted as happy as a kid with a new pair of fancy boots. A little later Steve left through the back door. I couldn't figure what for unless Mamie had sent him for something."

"To get killed," Corky Wills said sourly.

"That's what it was, all right," Bradford agreed. "When he didn't come back in a few minutes, I slipped out the back door to look for him. I found him not ten feet from the door with a knife sticking between his shoulders. He hadn't even had a chance to put up a fight."

"Ambushed!" Slim exclaimed, his blue eyes flashing.

"Dirty sneaking bushwhacker!" Corky Wills added.

Ferry looked straight at Corky. "That's a dirty way to die, isn't it?"

Corky glowered at Ferry for a moment; then his eyes dropped. Ferry realized that Steve Hayes' death was a serious blow to the Triangle F. But he couldn't help remembering the way Hayes and Corky had gloated over their ambushing of Otto Miller, the rancher who had ridden with the Leightons.

"I'm willing to bet my ranch against a Confederate dollar," Bradford went on, "that the whole thing was planned between Judd and Mamie. Otherwise Judd would have forced a showdown right there on the floor when Mamie ordered him out. Mamie found some excuse to send Steve out the back door. Judd was waiting for him. He never gave Steve a chance."

"They'll figure they've got us half licked now," Slim said grimly. "They must know that they got Pug yesterday in town. And Steve was the ramrod here. They probably think the rest of us will be pretty easy pickings."

"They'd better think again!" Ferry said after a moment of silence. "Slim, I'm making you foreman."

"Me?" The surprise on Slim's face gradually faded into a wide grin. "Won't I make some ramrod?"

"At least I figure you'll take orders," Ferry said.

"How about me handing out some orders?" Slim said, looking at Ferry.

"Such as?"

Slim jerked a thumb at the door. "You finishing your breakfast, then putting in a few hours practicing with that gun. You say we're not licked yet. If you want to make that a fact, you're going to have to get real handy with that gun of yours. You took on a man-sized job yesterday when you sent word to Judd Leighton that you were going to give him the fight he's been spoiling for."

Ferry grinned. "You see? You're beginning to sound like a ramrod already."

The lesson that day was the longest and hardest one Ferry had taken. Slim worked with him as though his life depended on his becoming an expert before the sun went down.

The ammunition Ferry had brought along vanished, and he glanced up at the sun which was beginning to burn.

"Looks like the end of our lesson, Slim."

Slim grinned. "You're not ready for graduation yet."

"We're out of ammunition. Can't shoot rocks."

"I've got more shells back in my saddle bags. I figured you might try to get out of work by shooting up all the shells you brought."

"Take it easy, Slim," Ferry complained. "Rome wasn't built in a day, you know."

Slim grinned again. "You're not Rome, either." His face sobered. "You may not have more than a day to learn your lesson, Dan. Hard to say when you'll have to take your test. If you flunk it the first time, you won't get a second chance."

Ferry nodded. "All right. I guess I can stand it a while longer if you can."

"I can," Slim said. "I'll get that box of shells."

Slim disappeared into the trees toward the horses he and Ferry had ridden out from the ranch. Ferry watched him go, then turned to stare idly down the valley.

A twig behind him snapped, and he spun around. Slim surely hadn't yet had time to get to the horses and come back. The green-broke horse Slim was riding today was still gun shy, so they had tied both horses far enough away from the target area to keep them from getting nervous.

Ferry froze in his tracks as he faced the two men who had moved into the clearing behind his back. The smaller of the two men had a gun trained on Ferry.

"Howdy, Ferry," the man said, his face spread in an evil grin.

Ferry was silent for a moment as he got a firm grip on his composure. "Howdy, Jake," he said.

Jake nodded. "So you remember me?"

"I'm not liable to forget a Leighton," Ferry said.

Jake laughed coarsely. "I reckon not. You're going to get a chance to get a lot better acquainted."

"Shut up, Jake," the other man said. "Get his gun and let's get going."

Ferry switched his gaze to Jake's twin, Jule. A little bigger than Jake, he wasn't given to much talk. A much more dangerous man than Jake, too, Slim had said. Ferry didn't doubt it. Jake was the talker. Jule did his talking with action.

Jake stepped close to Ferry and lifted his gun from its holster, and Ferry realized the significance of the move. He wasn't to be shot down here as he had expected when he first saw the twins. If they had planned to murder him, they wouldn't have bothered to take his gun first.

"Hey, Jule," Jake exclaimed as he spun the cylinder in Ferry's gun. "There ain't no shells in this thing." He turned to Ferry. "We heard shooting. That's how we found you so easy."

Ferry shrugged. "How would you expect a gun to get empty except by shooting?"

Jake laughed. "Corraling a tenderfoot when he's heeled is easy enough, but we walk in on one with no ammunition."

"Shut up, Jake!" Jule snapped. "Let's go."

Ferry was adding things up rapidly. For some reason, the Leightons wanted him as a prisoner.

Ferry was facing the dim trail by which Slim had gone to get the box of ammunition. Now, just as he was about to take a step in obedience to Jule's order, he caught a movement on the trail. Slim was coming back. He had to warn Slim or he'd walk into a trap, too.

"Let Jake talk all he wants," Ferry said, and laughed loudly as if he thought that was a big joke.

Ferry saw Slim jerk to a halt, then vanish into the trees at the side of the trail.

Jake stepped up in front of Ferry. "That ain't funny!" he sneered. With his open palm, he slapped Ferry, snapping his head around.

"Cut it out!" Jule ordered. "We're not to touch him; just bring him over home." He moved up and prodded Ferry in the ribs. "Get going."

Slim appeared noiselessly at the edge of the clearing directly behind the twins. His gun was in his hand.

"What's the rush, boys?" he asked softly, yet the words carried across the glade with the clarity of a bell. The twins stiffened. "Don't turn around!" Slim's words were as sharp as needles now. "If you do, you'll meet a hot slug."

The Leightons showed their respect for Slim's gun by not moving.

"Looks like you came over the ridge looking for something," Slim said as he moved a few feet closer. "I hate to have you go back disappointed."

"Now hold on," Jake said, his voice shrill and unsteady. "We haven't hurt anybody."

"And you're not going to," Slim said, and his tone left no room for doubt.

"We weren't going to hurt Ferry," Jake argued, his voice falling into a whine.

"I suppose that gun you're holding is your way of shaking hands," Slim said acidly.

"We were just taking Ferry prisoner."

"Leaving the dirty work for Judd," Slim snapped. "I suppose you think I'll let you live if you whine loud enough."

Jake's face turned a sickly green. Jake and Jule were still both facing Ferry, while Slim was behind them a few yards. Jake was trembling from head to foot, his lips quivering as he begged for his life. Jule's expression hadn't changed since he'd come into the clearing. His face was still calm, set, as though carved from stone.

Ferry got a shock when he looked at Slim's face. It was no longer a happy, carefree face split with a friendly grin. The grin was still there, but now it was twisted to one side and sent a chill down Ferry's spine. Slim's usually laughing eyes were shining with excitement now, sparkling with the fire of a gunman, the fire that only killing could quench.

Slim motioned to one side with the muzzle of his gun. "Better get to one side, Dan."

"This is murder, Slim," Ferry said. Nevertheless, he moved quickly to one side.

"You wouldn't kill us in cold blood, would you?" Jake whimpered.

"Stop blubbering!" Jule snapped. Then he spoke softly to his twin. "You've got your gun in your hand. Use it. I'll back you up."

But the muzzle of Jake's gun, hanging toward the ground, didn't move. Slim, reminding Ferry of a crouching cougar, waited a long minute. Finally he dropped his own gun into its holster.

"All right, you yellow snakes! I'll give you a chance—which is more than you deserve. My hands are empty. What are you going to do about it?"

"Nothing," Jake whimpered. "Just let us go."

Jule swore at his brother. "You're no Leighton!" Then he whirled, his hand streaking for the gun at his hip. Only after he saw that his brother had opened the fight and there was no escape did Jake turn, bringing up the gun that he had held in his hand all the time.

But Jake's hesitation cost him dearly. At Jule's first move, Slim drew. The move was like lightning, it seemed to Ferry, standing to one side, powerless to help or hinder.

Slim's first shot was directed at Jule, the more dangerous of the two even though his gun had been holstered when he made his move. Jule, off balance from his quick turn, staggered back from the impact of Slim's bullet, his gun exploding harmlessly into the ground at his feet.

Jake's first shot, fired in wild hysteria, snapped harmlessly past Slim and buried itself in the trunk of a tree ten feet behind him. Before Jake could squeeze the trigger again, Slim's gun shifted. It bucked in the young gunman's hand, and Jake's gun was silenced.

Dan watched Slim advance until he was looking down at the twins. Slowly he holstered his gun, and the wild light faded from his eyes. Then Ferry watched Slim Walters, the gunman, slowly disappear, and Slim Walters, the fun-loving youngster, replace him.

"I reckon that's a fit way for them to go," Slim said softly. "They came into the world together and they went out the same way."

"Wasn't there any other way?" Ferry asked.

Slim shook his head. "So far as Jake was concerned, maybe there was. But not Jule. When I walked into this clearing it was a settled fact, as far as he was concerned, that one of us wasn't going to walk out. Get hold of yourself, Dan. Yesterday you sent word to Judd that he'd get war the way he wanted it. This is it."

Ferry nodded toward the bodies. "What are you going to do with them?"

"I'll find their horses," Slim said. "Got a piece of paper and a pencil?"

"I'll get some," Ferry said.

While Slim was gone, Ferry dug into his pockets and found a stub pencil and a scrap of paper. Slim came back with two Hooked J horses. In a few minutes he had the twins tied across the saddles of the horses, and he took the pencil and paper from Ferry.

For five minutes Slim labored over the paper, the pencil held rigidly in his hand. When he finished, he held the paper out to Ferry.

"That should explain things to them," he said.

Ferry ran his eyes over the paper, hesitating at times as he strove to make out the crude lettering.

> "This is what happens to mavericks that stray off their home range and try to get bossy. Any other maverick crossing the ridge will get branded the same way.
>
>   Slim Walters—foreman of the Triangle F"

Without a word, Ferry handed the note back to

Slim. Slim turned to the nearest Hooked J horse and, rolling the paper, tied it securely with one of the leather thongs behind the saddle. Then he looped the reins over the saddle horn and gave each horse a slap, sending it out of the clearing on the trail over the ridge.

XI

It seemed to Rosanne that the day after the celebration in Sundown was one of Nature's beautiful days.
Connie seemed to want to stay in the house during the
morning, but Rosanne guessed it was to avoid Link
Dalton. So it wasn't until after noon that they first
ventured outside. And that soon proved to be a mistake. Link Dalton was standing idly behind a tree a
short distance from the corral, and as the girls came
past him, he wheeled around in front of them. Connie
caught her breath in surprise.

"Having a nice walk?" Dalton asked easily.

"Up until now, yes," Rosanne said acidly.

"Don't be so touchy," Link grunted with a frown.
"I just want to ask a few questions. Then I'll let you
both alone."

"We'll appreciate that," Rosanne said.

Link ignored her and turned to Connie. Before he could say anything, Connie cut him off.

"The answers are still the same, Link," she said, her face white and tense.

"You're still saying you don't know anything?"

"I don't Link, honest. Jig Ailey never told me anything, and I didn't pry."

"You know more than you're telling," Link said, and there was an open threat in his voice. "You're going to tell me sometime. The sooner you talk, the easier it will be on you."

"You've asked your question, Link," Rosanne said sharply. "Now get out of the way."

Link shot a glance at Rosanne, then turned his green eyes back on Connie. "Think it over, Connie. Think it over good."

He moved aside, and Rosanne and Connie walked on toward the corral. Rosanne glanced back to see Link watching them like a cat watching a bird on a perch just above his head.

"Do you know something you didn't tell Link?" Rosanne asked.

Connie shook her head. "No. I told him all I know

about Jig Ailey and his mine. But I can't make him believe it."

Joe appeared at the barn door as they reached the corral. "Want a couple of horses saddled?" he asked.

"If you'll make it three," Connie said. "I'd rather have you along if we go for a ride."

Rosanne agreed. "So would I."

Joe started to turn back into the barn, then stopped, cocking an ear toward the trail leading down from Thunder Ridge. Rosanne heard it, too: the slow even thud of hoofbeats coming from behind the trees.

"That must be Jule and Jake," Joe said, coming out of the barn.

"Where have they been?" Rosanne asked.

"Over the ridge trying to pick up Ferry."

"What for?" Rosanne exclaimed. "Did Link send them?"

"Judd said he sent them," Joe said. "But I figure it was part of his deal with Link. I reckon Link figures he can make Ferry tell him things he can't find out any other way."

"If Link wanted Ferry, why didn't he go after him himself?" Rosanne demanded.

"He's not built that way," Joe said in disgust.

He swung away from the barn and headed for the far end of the corral where the trail from the ridge ended. Judd came from the back of the house to join him.

Rosanne and Connie waited at the barn for Joe to come back.

"There comes Joe," Connie said suddenly. "And there's nobody with him."

Rosanne, catching the look on Joe's face as he came closer, ran out to meet him. "What's wrong, Joe?"

Joe cleared his throat, but no words came. Silently he handed her a piece of paper. Rosanne read it, with Connie looking over her shoulder.

"Then—then—Jule and Jake—?" Something choked the words in Rosanne's throat.

Joe nodded. "Yeah. They ran into Slim Walters instead of Ferry." A savage gleam shone through the mist that clung to his eyelashes. "That was Dalton's idea to send them over there! He'll pay for that!"

Others of the Leighton followers had fallen in this war, but Rosanne's grief had been only a temporary shock and her anger had soon superseded the grief. But the loss of two of her four brothers in one blow struck far too deep for anger to relieve the grief.

"Maw will rave like mad when she finds out," Joe said softly. "You don't want to be there then, do you?"

"Maybe I can help," Rosanne said.

"Nobody can help Maw now. She won't cry like most mothers. She'll rave and swear to kill every man on Ferry's ranch. You can't help a woman like that till she calms down. Why don't you and Connie ride up on the ridge? I'll be along in a few minutes, as soon as things settle down a little."

Rosanne waited till Joe had two horses saddled; then she and Connie mounted and rode around the corral and up the trail toward the crest of Thunder Ridge.

It was peaceful on the ridge. The sun was already past its crest, but it was still hot enough to keep most of the birds silent in their shady nooks.

Rosanne tried to keep her mind on the little things that so often had occupied her thoughts when she was up on the ridge. But today those things seemed out of place. The peacefulness of the ridge was only a mockery.

"What was that?" Connie asked suddenly, bringing Rosanne out of her gloomy thoughts.

Rosanne looked at Connie, then wheeled to face the direction from which they had come. Link Dalton was riding a horse into the clearing, his green eyes bright with confidence.

"What are you doing here?" Rosanne demanded.

"I saw you girls starting out for a ride and thought you might get lonesome, so I came along for company."

"We don't need your company!" Rosanne snapped.

Dalton's grin faded; his yellow-green eyes gleamed above his crooked nose. "I won't be bothering you long if Connie will tell me where that mine is."

"I've told you I don't know," Connie said, almost in tears.

"And I don't believe you." Dalton dismounted, staring at Connie with the steadiness of an angry rattler. When she kept silent, he slid his gun from its holster. "You'll tell me or I'll make you wish you had!"

"You fool!" Rosanne snapped. "Put that gun away!"

"I know what I'm doing," Dalton said. "You've got just ten seconds to start talking, Connie."

"I've already told you everything I know," Connie said in desperation.

"All right," Dalton said, and there was a note of finality in his voice that made Rosanne shiver. "I'm going to take you to a place where your memory will be better."

Connie gasped and clutched the horn of her saddle. A deep fury gripped Rosanne, and her hand dropped to her .38. But Dalton caught the move and his gun swung around.

"Don't try that! I'm not above shooting a woman if she starts slinging lead my way."

"I'll bet you're not!" Rosanne snapped. But her hand came away from the gun. "You're lower than a snake, Link Dalton!"

Dalton moved over to flip Rosanne's gun out of the holster. "Words aren't going to hurt anybody. Might as well save them." He backed to his horse and took some short pieces of rope from the saddle bag. "I was expecting to have to do this, so I came prepared. Put your hands behind your back, Connie."

"You low-down yellow-bellied coward!" Rosanne burst out. "Aren't you man enough to keep a girl prisoner without tying her?"

"I'm not taking just one," Dalton said. "I'm not fool enough to let you run back and tell everybody what happened to Connie."

Dalton started toward Connie. When his back was

half turned to Rosanne, she wheeled her horse toward the trail down to the Hooked J. But before she could dig in her heels, Dalton spun around, his gun centered on Rosanne.

"Hold it, my pretty lady," he said sharply. "Two of your family killed in one day is enough, don't you think? You'll wait your turn. I won't neglect you."

Seething with helpless fury, Rosanne sat in rigid silence while Dalton tied Connie's hands behind her back. Then he came across to her. She kicked at him as he approached, but he only laughed. When she kicked again, he slapped the barrel of his gun across her boot. The sharp pain brought a gasp from her lips.

"Now then maybe you'll behave," Dalton snapped. "I've got only so much patience, and you've about worn it out."

He jerked her hands behind her back and wound the rope around her wrists, jerking it so tightly she wondered if any blood could circulate through her hands.

"Just wait till Joe finds out about this!" Rosanne raged.

"I'll wait," Dalton said easily. "When he finds out, we'll be a long way from here in a place Joe will never think of looking."

"Where?"

"Secret Valley." Dalton scowled at Connie. "Maybe your memory will be better there. Connie, you take the lead, Rosanne next, and I'll come along behind."

While Dalton was mounting, Rosanne shot a glance down the trail toward the Hooked J. Joe was nowhere in sight. Then Dalton started the horses down a dim winding trail on the Triangle F side of Thunder Ridge. This little used trail angled gently down the slope, coming out in the valley a mile above the Triangle F ranch buildings.

Rosanne knew she had to leave some kind of sign for Joe to follow. The trail cut through an aspen grove where small trees had pushed branches out over the trail, almost blocking it. Rosanne deliberately kneed her horse to one side, where he smashed against some of those new limbs. Two or three of them broke under the weight. Dalton swore and prodded Rosanne's horse back into the trail.

A half-mile farther on, Rosanne repeated the maneuver and again broke some limbs. Joe was a good tracker. He should be able to follow a trail like that. But what if he didn't see it?

"How long are you going to keep us up there?"

Rosanne demanded.

"Till Connie tells me what I want to know," Dalton said. "That may be an hour, or it may be a week. That's up to Connie."

XII

Dan Ferry went to the corral and saddled Jupiter without telling anyone when to expect him back. His plans were vague. He just needed to get away to do some thinking, and that lookout promontory up the valley seemed like the ideal place.

The sun was well past its zenith when Ferry headed the big white horse into the trail leading up the valley. In the back of his mind was the possibility that he might see the black horse with the white belt over its hips.

As he came to the open parks along the bank of the creek, he scanned the ground for fresh tracks. He was amazed when he found tracks the first time he looked. That first glance also told him that the tracks hadn't been made by one horse. Two or maybe three horses had been along there very recently.

Ferry reined off toward the base of the lookout.

He left Jupiter in a thicket at the base of the promontory and climbed hastily to the top. After sprawling full length under a tree for a few minutes to catch his breath, Ferry moved out to the point where he had an unobstructed view of the valley in both directions.

He uncased his binoculars and began scanning the open parks and the trail, where he could see it through the trees. But it was an hour before his vigilance was rewarded. And then it was at the upper end of the valley in the trough that led over the ridge into Secret Valley.

He experienced a shock as he realized that someone else knew how to get into Secret Valley. He could see three horses going up that steep trail, but they were so far away that, even with his powerful glasses, Ferry couldn't tell much about the riders.

He watched them closely as they climbed into the trough and the freakish winds struck them. The hats of the two lead riders flipped off their heads and hung down their backs. The sun caught the light hair of the lead rider and reflected it like gold.

Ferry whistled softly. The rider was a girl. A moment later he realized that the second rider with the black hair was also a girl. He steadied his glasses, tense and excited now. The rear rider ducked his head into the wind and didn't lose his hat. Ferry recalled how cold those blasts of wind were and wondered why the two girls didn't put their hats back on.

A possible solution struck him as the riders moved on and the girls seemed to make no move to ride more comfortably or to allow for the blasts of wind. Maybe they couldn't.

After another minute spent studying the three riders, he was convinced that the girls couldn't use their hands. They were prisoners.

He cased his glasses and hurried back down the steep trail to his horse. Regardless of who was taking the girls into the valley or what his reason might be for doing it, the fact was clear to Ferry that the girls needed help. And he required no prodding to accept the job of trying to provide that help.

The big white horse seemed to catch something of the impatience of his rider as he tore through the trees to the trail, then leveled into a long-legged gallop. As they raced across each clearing, Ferry looked ahead to see if there was any movement in the trough, although he really didn't expect any. Whoever had taken the girls into the valley wasn't likely to bring them out again right away.

As he started up the rocky trough, he kept searching the trail ahead of him, knowing that if there was an ambush, he would have little chance of avoiding it. But he reached the top of the trough without mishap and moved cautiously ahead, his gun balanced in his hand on the horn of his saddle.

He shivered as the first freezing blast of wind struck him and ducked his head, pulling his hat lower. He kept on the alert as his horse wound around the corners of the old water course. But he saw nothing till he broke out of the winding passage and halted where he could look out over the huge pocket that was Secret Valley.

There seemed to be no sign of life below him. But he knew that was deceiving. Three riders had come in there. They couldn't have gotten out any way but over the trail he had just used. Then he caught the faint aroma of wood smoke and saw a thin wisp of it curling above the treetops in the direction of the cabin.

He nudged Jupiter down the trail, glad that it was out of sight of the cabin but still feeling like a mountain-sized target. Relief swept over him when he got to the bottom of the trail and reined the big white horse into the trees at the base of the wall.

He rode forward for a short distance, then dismounted and tied Jupiter's reins to a small tree. On foot, he moved cautiously toward the cabin. When he came in sight of it, it appeared deserted except for the smoke curling lazily out of the chimney.

Dodging from tree to tree, he reached a point only about twenty yards from the door without being challenged. The door was open, but from his angle, Ferry couldn't see inside. Surprise was his chief weapon, and the longer he hesitated, the more chance there was that he would lose that. If someone in the cabin happened to see him or if Jupiter decided suddenly to whistle a greeting to the other horse in the valley, Ferry's chances of getting into the cabin alive would become mighty slim.

Gripping his gun, he suddenly broke from cover and dashed for the door. There wasn't a sound except the pounding of his running feet. He hit the threshold and plunged inside, his gun sweeping the room, looking for a target.

For a second there wasn't a sound inside the cabin.

Then two voices chorused his name. Ferry's eyes, rapidly adjusting to the gloomy interior, located the girls at the far end of the cabin. An angry exclamation burst from him as he saw that they were bound hand and foot.

"Who's responsible for this?" he demanded.

"Link Dalton!" Rosanne said, spitting the words out like poison pellets.

"Where is he now?"

"After water. He'll be back any second."

Ferry turned to look out the door. "I'll wait for him." He started back to the girls. "I'll get you out of those ropes. Maybe you'd like to help me."

"There's nothing I'd like better!" Rosanne said fiercely.

"We'll have to surprise him," Connie said. "If we don't—"

She let the words die as running footsteps sounded outside. Ferry whirled around and leaped for the front of the cabin, pressing against the wall just to one side of the door.

He barely made it before a man burst into the cabin, a gun in his hand, and halted in the center of the room. Sight of the gun convinced Ferry that he had been detected. He knew he had only a second to act.

"Drop that gun, Dalton!" he said sharply.

Instead of dropping the gun, the man wheeled toward Ferry, his gun swinging in line. Ferry fired, at the last split-second his gun veering toward the man's shoulder. He had been sure he wanted to kill Link Dalton, but when the moment of decision came, he couldn't bring himself to kill a man.

Then, as the echo of his shot rocked the room, he realized with a sickening shock that he had made a mistake. The man whirling toward him wasn't Link Dalton. If he hadn't been so certain it would be Dalton, he would probably have seen that this man was taller and not so heavy. This was Joe Leighton.

Ferry heard both girls scream as Joe crumpled to the floor like an empty sack, his gun clattering away. But the next instant, Joe was up on his knees reaching for his gun with his other hand.

"I'll get you, Dalton!" he screamed.

"Hold it!" Ferry yelled. "I'm not Dalton." Then, as Joe stopped and blinked uncertainly at him, he reached down and scooped up Joe's gun. "Dalton is outside. We'll have him to deal with yet—if you're not set on finishing me first."

Joe Leighton propped himself up on one elbow and stared at Ferry. "Dan Ferry!" he muttered at last. "Why don't you finish the job you started?"

"I thought you were Dalton," Ferry said.

Ferry ran across the room to the girls, slashing the ropes that held them.

"See what you can do for Joe's shoulder," he said. "I'll keep an eye out for Dalton. He'll come running now."

He hurried back to the door and kicked it shut, leaving only a crack through which he could see. The door had barely closed when a bullet thudded into it. Link Dalton had them bottled up, and now he was driving in the cork.

Ferry snapped a shot back in the general direction of Dalton, then turned to the girls, who were helping Joe to a position along the wall.

"Where's he hit?"

Rosanne looked up. "In the shoulder. I can't tell how bad. I need some water to wash it."

"Link was bringing water," Connie said in despair.

"Sorry about the shoulder, Joe," Ferry said.

Joe looked at him, pain and bewilderment clouding his eyes. "If you were anybody but Dan Ferry, I might believe that," he said slowly. "I reckon you did think I was Dalton, all right."

Ferry snapped another shot through the crack in the door. "Think he'll try to barge in here?"

"No," Joe grunted. "He's yellow. He won't crowd us as long as anybody here is able to shoot."

Rosanne hurried into the little room at the back of the cabin and returned with an old sheet. She and Connie ripped this up and bandaged Joe's shoulder. Ferry exchanged some shots with Dalton, but he soon backed away from the door. A lucky shot might tag him there. His chances of hitting Dalton, concealed as he was behind some trees and big rocks, were too slim to make the effort worth the risk.

"Looks like Dalton holds the trump cards now," he said. "We'll wait till dark. That won't be long now. Maybe we can make a break then. How's Joe?"

"He's holding out pretty well," Rosanne said. "We need water mighty bad."

"We'll get it after dark," Ferry said.

"You'll get plugged if you go out that door," Joe said, his voice tight with pain. "I wouldn't lose any sleep over that. But what will happen to Sis and Connie if you cash in?"

"If it comes to a pinch, you can still handle a gun, can't you?" Ferry asked.

"Maybe. But I'm not much good with a busted wing."

Darkness came quickly as the sun dropped behind the snowcapped peaks to the west. As dusk settled over the cabin, Ferry crouched close to the door, weighing his chances of making a break through the door. He hadn't heard from Dalton for some time now, but he knew he was still out there.

Ferry glanced occasionally across toward Rosanne and Connie, who were trying to make Joe more comfortable.

"It's awfully quiet outside," Connie said, getting up and moving around nervously.

"It is, all right," Ferry said, nudging the door open another inch. He couldn't see much out there but the full moon just reaching up over the eastern rim of the valley would soon bathe the whole valley in light. He'd have to make his break in the next few minutes before the moon turned the night into day.

Then suddenly Ferry twitched his nose, alarm racing through his whole body. "Do you smell smoke?"

"Yes, I do," Connie said, her voice suddenly close

to hysteria.

Ferry left his post and dashed into the back room. There the smell of smoke was twice as strong. It seemed to be seeping between the logs along one whole side of the bedroom. He hurried back to the main room.

"What is it?" Rosanne asked, the calmness in her voice in sharp contrast to Connie's.

There was nothing to be gained by postponing the inevitable. "It's the cabin," he said. "Dalton has set fire to it."

Ferry expected Connie to collapse into hysterics. But she only gasped and leaned against the table. Rosanne's voice was barely above a whisper when she spoke.

"What can we do?"

"No water to put it out," Ferry said. "We'll have to get set to make a break."

"Going to roast us alive!" Joe swore. "That dirty side-winder!"

Joe's words were punctured by a rifle shot, the bullet thudding into the door again. But the shot came from a different angle from before and was much closer to the cabin.

No one said anything. The rifle had said all that needed to be said. They were in a burning trap, and Dalton intended to see that they stayed there.

Smoke was curling into the main room now through the partition doorway. The girls started to cough. A weird light came from the rear of the cabin as flames leaped into being and licked up the tinder-dry wall.

Ferry called the girls to the tiny opening in the wall that served as a window.

"You can get air here," Ferry said. "I'll help Joe over."

Ferry crossed the room in the uncanny light. Joe was already on his feet.

"I can manage all right," Joe said. "How do we get out?"

"There's only one way. How long can you hold out in here?"

"Not more than a week!" Joe snorted. "You can't get out that door. Don't try it."

"I don't figure on being roasted in here," Ferry said. "If I make it, I'll warm things up for Dalton; then you and the girls can get out. If I don't get out, you'll have to make the next try."

"I'll make the first try," Joe said. "I'm only half

a man, anyway."

"You'll wait!" Ferry said sharply. "If one of us gets out, he's got to be in shape to give Dalton a battle."

Ferry moved across to the door. The whole rear of the cabin was ablaze, forming a background of light that would silhouette any target as it came through the door. But the smoke was clearing in the room now, the heat driving it up through a hole already burned in the roof.

Ferry kicked the door open and dodged back. A bullet snapped through the opening. Ferry lifted his gun from its holster and took a firm grip around the cylinder and over the trigger guard. By the flickering light of the fire, he picked a tree some twenty feet from the door. Just as he was taking a deep breath for his plunge into the open, he heard Rosanne's words from across the room.

"Good luck, Dan!"

The roar of the fire swelled to whip the words away. But it couldn't wipe out the surge of confidence that swept over him. He took off his hat and waved it in the doorway. A bullet ripped at it. The next instant Ferry catapulted through the opening.

XIII

Ferry made three long leaps before throwing himself into a ball and rolling toward the safety of the tree he had picked before leaving the door. One bullet snapped past his head before he hit the dirt, and another kicked up pine needles a foot behind him as he rolled.

Then he was at the tree and quickly backed into it, leaving Link Dalton no target. Ferry was sure that Dalton had been set to blast the first target to show itself in the doorway. He had fired that shot at Ferry's hat. After that set shot had been wasted, Dalton had fired in a frenzy, aiming only by chance.

Ferry got to his feet, answering the flash of Dalton's gun with bullets of his own. After a couple of even exchanges, Dalton abandoned his post and retreated.

Faced with an even fight, Dalton apparently had no stomach for seeing the battle through.

Ferry dodged through the trees, trying to keep a line on Dalton's retreat. At first Dalton helped by firing a shot his way now and then as he ran. But then he stopped firing entirely, and the only way Ferry could keep track of his retreat was to stop and listen.

Then, after a minute of quiet when Ferry thought he had lost Dalton completely, the thunder of hoofbeats as a horse was suddenly kicked into a gallop echoed through the valley. Ferry stopped running and turned back toward the burning cabin. Flames were leaping from the entire roof now, and Ferry broke into a run.

He found Joe and the girls already outside. He leaned against a tree, trying to catch his breath.

"Is he gone?" Rosanne asked.

Ferry nodded. "I heard him riding away. I doubt he'll stop till he's out of the valley."

"You can bet he won't," Joe said. "Let's have some water."

Ferry pushed away from the tree. "I'll get my canteen." He glanced around the area. "This looks like a good place to bed down."

He saw a look of dismay flash across Connie's face. But he didn't stop to explain. Joe needed water. In a couple of minutes he was back with his canteen.

"Empty this," he said. "I'll get some more from the creek. Then I'll bring the saddle blankets. We shouldn't be too uncomfortable this close to that fire."

"Can't we go home tonight?" Connie asked.

"I'm afraid not," Ferry said. "That trough on the other side of the ridge is bad enough to travel in daylight."

"But Link Dalton is going over it, isn't he? Surely we can make it."

"We could," Ferry admitted. "But Joe couldn't."

That put an end to objections to spending the night in the valley. After Joe had been given a drink and his wound washed out and bandaged again, Ferry spread out the saddle blankets he had taken from the four horses, giving the girls one each and putting two on Joe.

"What about you?" Rosanne asked.

"I won't be sleeping much," Ferry said. "There's a chance that Dalton didn't leave the valley."

Within minutes the little clearing a short distance from the cabin was quiet. The fire burned out, the height of the flames sinking rapidly as the fuel ran out.

When the girls awoke, the snow on the peaks at the western end of the valley was glistening with the first rays of the morning sun. Down in the lower end of the valley, deep in the shadow of the eastern wall, it was still only half light as the girls turned their first waking thoughts to the welfare of Joe.

"How is he?" Ferry asked.

"Seems to be pretty well," Rosanne said. She tipped her head back and shook it, letting her raven hair fall in waves down her back. "Now how about breakfast?" Her laugh was low and soft, like the ripple of the stream behind them.

Ferry grinned. "I'm afraid any breakfast we might have had was up in the cabin, and it got slightly overdone."

Joe tossed back his blankets, wincing with pain. "Then let's travel," he said.

"I'll saddle up," Ferry said, and picked up the saddle blankets.

Ten minutes later they were filing slowly out of the grassy clearing where they had spent the night. Not one of them had more than glanced through the trees

at the pile of smoldering rubble that had been Jig
Ailey's cabin and had almost become their crematory.
The sooner they could forget that experience the bet-
ter they would like it.

Ferry led the way on the trail that climbed steeply
up the east wall of the valley. He glanced back at Joe,
who was staying in his saddle with an effort. His
bloody shirt front testified to the loss of blood he had
sustained. It would be a miracle, Ferry decided, if
Joe could ride all the way home. It would be a tough
ride for a healthy man.

In the trough at the top of the pass over the ridge,
Ferry reined back to Joe. Dismounting, he handed
Jupiter's reins to Rosanne.

"You lead him down," he said. "I'll steady Joe."

No one argued his decision. It was obvious that this
was the only way Joe was going to make it to the bottom of the trough. Then there would be several miles
of riding plus the climb over Thunder Ridge before
Joe would be home.

It was slow going down the trough. Ferry had to
keep one hand on Joe to steady him as his horse slowly picked his way down the steep trail. Joe hung on
with grim determination and insisted on riding alone

after they reached the bottom of the trough.

But by the time they came to the fork in the trail where it divided, one branch running on down the valley to the Triangle F and the other climbing at an angle to the top of Thunder Ridge, Joe was barely able to stay in the saddle.

"I'm afraid we'll never get him home," Rosanne said softly, dropping back beside Ferry and Joe.

"He's tuckered, all right," Ferry agreed. "He should be in bed instead of in a saddle."

"I've got a proposition to make to you, Dan," Rosanne said suddenly, her face set with determination.

Ferry looked at her sharply. "I'm listening."

"If you'll help us get Joe home, I'll guarantee your safety while you're there."

"Can you guarantee that?"

She bit her underlip. "I'll do my best. I won't deny you'll be taking a big risk."

Ferry nodded. "I'll take the chance."

"I'll get home myself some way," Joe mumbled thickly. "Judd will kill you, Ferry."

"I doubt if Rosanne and Connie can hold you in your saddle down Thunder Ridge," Ferry said.

A worried frown creased Rosanne's forehead. "I can only guarantee what I can control, Dan," she said.

"I'll take a chance on the rest," Ferry said.

It was well past noon when the little caravan reached the top of Thunder Ridge. The long climb along the slope to reach the big rock had taken what little strength Joe had left. As they started down the steep trail to the Hooked J buildings, Ferry had to support Joe in the saddle. Every step the horse took threatened to unseat him. Ferry knew that neither Rosanne nor Connie could have kept Joe on his horse.

They came out of the trail behind the corral and, skirting this, stopped in front of the yard gate. Rosanne and Connie dropped out of their saddles and came around to help Ferry lift Joe off his horse. Joe collapsed in Ferry's arms and Ferry lifted him, striding through the gate toward the house.

Mrs. Leighton, her black hair straggling down over her face, appeared on the porch. "What happened to Joe?" she demanded, her voice harsh and bitter.

"Joe was shot in the shoulder," Rosanne explained quickly. "He's weak from bleeding so much."

"Who's the fellow carrying him?" Mrs. Leighton demanded suspiciously.

"Dan Ferry," Rosanne said. "He practically saved Joe's life."

"Ferry!" Mrs. Leighton screamed. "You let a Ferry come on this place? I'll kill him myself!" She whirled toward the door.

But Rosanne was there before her, blocking the doorway. "Maw!" she said with such sharpness that Mrs. Leighton stopped in amazement. "I asked Dan Ferry to come here. Connie and I couldn't get Joe home alone. I promised him he'd be safe while he was here and I'm going to see that he is!"

Mrs. Leighton stared at her daughter as if hypnotized. She stepped aside in a daze and let Ferry carry Joe through the door. Ferry followed Rosanne into a small room where a bed occupied the space along one wall. Ferry laid Joe on the bed, then turned to Rosanne.

"We'd better get that shirt off. I'm afraid the jolting he got coming down the ridge has opened the wound again."

As Rosanne and Connie began working over Joe, he stirred weakly. Ferry had thought he was unconscious, but now his eyes opened.

"Just let me rest," he said.

Mrs. Leighton appeared in the doorway with her husband behind her. Jasper Leighton still had his arm in a dirty sling.

"Now I want to know what happened!" Mrs. Leighton demanded. "Why did you let this killer come here? What happened to Joe? Who shot him? Rosanne, do you hear me?"

Ferry turned to face the older Leightons, but before he could say a word, Rosanne stepped in front of him and pushed him back, shielding him.

"Link Dalton kidnapped Connie and me and took us to Secret Valley," Rosanne said. "I left a trail for Joe and he followed us. But before he got there, Dan Ferry came. He had seen us go over the wall into the valley and came to get us away from Link. Link had gone after water when Dan rushed into the cabin. We heard footsteps and thought it was Link coming back. When he dashed in, Dan yelled at him to drop his gun. But he didn't. He turned to shoot, and Dan shot him. Only it wasn't Link Dalton; it was Joe."

"Ferry shot Joe?" Mrs. Leighton's face turned reddish purple in her rage.

"Couldn't he see the difference?" Jasper Leighton asked more calmly. "Joe and Dalton don't look alike."

"There wasn't time," Rosanne said quickly. "Connie and I saw it was Joe, but before we could say a word, it was all over. Both Joe and Dan Ferry thought the other was Dalton. Later Dalton burned the cabin, trying to burn us out. Dan broke out, nearly getting shot, and drove Link away so we could get out. Then he helped us get Joe home. He did all he could for us, and I promised him his safety while he is here."

"I wouldn't promise a Ferry anything but a bullet!" Mrs. Leighton raged, then wheeled and left the room, Jasper tagging along behind her.

"You'd better go now," Rosanne said as soon as her mother was out of hearing. "The way Maw is acting, she might be one of the things I can't control."

Ferry looked at Joe's shoulder. The shirt was gone and he could see that the wound was inflamed. "Be a good idea to have a doc look at that," he said."

"I'm going to ride into Sundown pretty soon. I'll bring Doc Robson out."

A step sounded at the door behind Ferry, and he whirled toward it. Judd was standing there, a gun in his hand.

"Glad you turned around, Ferry," Judd said, his eyes bright with anticipation. "I hate to shoot a man in the back."

"No, Judd!" Rosanne screamed.

"Get back!" Judd yelled.

Ferry braced himself for the shock of a bullet. He knew Judd was going to shoot. Ferry had a gun on his hip, but it might as well have been over the ridge at the Triangle F.

The gun roared, but Judd had waited just a fraction of a second too long. Rosanne had thrown herself at him, knocking his gun arm down. The bullet plowed into the floor three inches in front of Ferry. Acrid smoke filled the room.

It was Ferry's chance and he knew it. He could draw now and be on even terms with Judd when Rosanne let go. But he couldn't seem to make himself move. He had come there under a truce. He couldn't kill a Leighton in his own house.

Judd shoved Rosanne back and stepped to one side, bringing up the gun again. But Rosanne reacted instantly, leaping in front of Ferry and facing Judd.

"Get out of the way, Rosanne!" Judd yelled. "If you don't, I'll drill you both!"

"Dan Ferry is here because I asked him to come," Rosanne said. "I promised him he'd be safe."

"He'll find out you're not boss here."

"He helped bring Joe home."

"He shot him first!" Judd snapped. "Maw told me. Now I'm going to even the score. Get out of the way!"

"I won't do it!" Rosanne said, standing her ground.

Anger flushed Judd's face, adding to the hatred already there. "If that's the way you want it, you can have it."

For an instant time hung suspended as Judd made his decision whether or not to carry out his threat and kill his own sister to get to Dan Ferry. Ferry started to move to one side where Rosanne would be safe from the maniacal hatred driving Judd. But a movement on the bed behind him arrested his action.

"Drop that gun, Judd!"

Joe's voice was weak, but there was no mistaking the determination in it. Judd stared at Joe, his jaw sagging. Ferry stole a glance at Joe. Somehow Joe had reached his gun, which had been hanging in its holster over the head of the bed where Rosanne had put it. Now he had it in his left hand, trained unwaveringly on Judd's belt buckle.

"You bucking me, too?" Judd asked in amazement.

"You heard Sis," Joe said. "Ferry is here on a

truce. She guaranteed his safety, and he's going to get it."

"You wouldn't shoot your own brother," Judd said confidently, some of his dominance returning.

"Try me and see."

Joe's voice was weak, but not even Judd could doubt the strength of his determination. Slowly Judd opened his fingers, and the gun thudded to the floor. Rosanne scooped it up.

"Now get out of here!" Joe said, his voice sinking to a whisper.

Judd backed to the doorway, the purple veins standing out in his neck. "You'll be sorry you did that, Joe Leighton! As for you, Ferry, you won't live another day! I promise that!"

He wheeled and disappeared into the other room.

XIV

Dan Ferry's mind was whirling as he rode down off Thunder Ridge.

Halfway down the steep slope, the trail came out on a narrow ledge which was fairly free of trees. Ferry reined in Jupiter to give him a rest. As his eyes wandered up the valley behind the ranch toward Secret Valley, his mind on what had happened there last night, his attention was caught by a movement on the trail along the creek.

Whipping out his binoculars, he focused them hurriedly. His first look with his naked eye hadn't deceived him. It was a rider on an oddly marked horse, a black horse with a white belt over his hips, the same he had seen that first day he had been up in the valley. He had thought the rider was following him that day.

Today the rider was going away from him.

He studied the rider closely. His back was to Ferry, and the distance was too great to determine much about him. But it was too small a man to be Judd Leighton or Dalton.

Ferry nudged Jupiter into motion again. As Ferry broke out of the trees at the base of the ridge, Slim met him.

"Some ride you took yesterday," Slim said calmly, his curious eyes on Ferry.

"Been a long one with nothing to eat," Ferry said.

"Wong Ling has gone to town in the buckboard for supplies," Slim said. "But I reckon we can round up some grub."

Slim didn't press for an explanation of Ferry's absence, but Ferry knew it was the one thing Slim and the two remaining Triangle F hands, Lige Conklin and Corky Wills, wanted to hear. So, as he ate the food Slim found in the kitchen cupboards, he told the three men what had happened since he had left the ranch the previous afternoon.

"I remember the old man mentioning Dalton," Slim said. "He worked here before we came, I guess. The old man fired him. He tried to burn you alive, did he? I'm going to enjoy evening the score with him."

"I've got a hunch we've got problems we're going to have to take care of before Dalton," Corky Wills said. "What was that threat you said Judd made?"

"He said I wouldn't live another day," Ferry said.

"He's not given to making promises he doesn't keep," Lige Conklin said.

"Lige is right," Slim added. "Judd's busy right now thinking up some way to kill you, Dan. I'll bet on that."

Ferry nodded. "I don't doubt it. What will he dream up?"

"Whatever we'd least expect," Corky said.

"What's that?" Ferry asked.

"That he'd come right over here after you," Slim said promptly. "He's alone now that Joe is wounded and the twins are dead—unless he picks up Dalton."

"Are you counting Belcher and his deputies?" Ferry asked.

Slim scratched his head. "Reckon not. But Belcher isn't much for anybody to count on, even Judd."

"It does look crazy for Judd to ride in on us, doesn't it?" Ferry said thoughtfully. "Then that's just what we'd better get ready for."

As if in direct answer to Ferry's prediction, the Triangle F wagon came rocking down the road from town, the Chinese cook, Wong Ling, standing up in the front, lashing the horses at every other jump.

"What's chewing on his tail?" Slim demanded, running out to the veranda. "Maybe Judd's coming now."

Lige ran out and helped the cook bring the team to a stop. Ferry led Slim and Corky out to the cook.

"Who's after you?" Ferry demanded.

"Nobody yet," the cook said. "Leighton feller in town. Guns all over horses. Coming here, I think."

"Just Judd alone?" Slim asked.

"Sheriff, many deputies with him."

Slim turned to Ferry. "Guess you called the turn, Dan. Now they'll outnumber us, two to one."

"But they'll probably figure on surprising us, which they won't."

"Were they ready to leave town when you left?" Slim asked.

"In saloon," Wong Ling said, starting to unload his groceries. "Drink up courage."

"That figures," Slim said. "If it was just Judd and

fellows like him, they wouldn't have stopped at the saloon. But Belcher will want the free whiskey. And he'll need some kind of false nerve. He doesn't have any of his own. I'd guess we've got maybe an hour, Dan."

Ferry turned to look at the bunkhouse standing only ten feet from the side door of the house. "We'll have to defend both buildings," he said thoughtfully. "Can't let them move into one while we're in the other. Slim, you divide the guns and ammunition between the two buildings."

"Sure," Slim said. "Corky and I will hold down the bunkhouse while you and Lige keep them away from the house. I figure Hugh Bradford will be along, too. He's not one to miss a fight."

"This isn't his scrap," Ferry said.

"That's not the way Hugh will see it. This looks like it ought to be a honey of a fight." Slim rubbed his hands in anticipation.

"Do we have any sacks?" Ferry asked.

"A couple of dozen in the back of the bunkhouse," Lige said.

"Get them and a shovel. We'll sack up some sand to use for breastworks."

Lige and Corky disappeared into the bunkhouse and came out with a shovel and two armfuls of sacks. Slim went into the house after the guns and ammunition. Ferry led the way to the creek, where a sandy beach several feet wide bordered the stream.

It took nearly an hour to get the two buildings barricaded to Ferry's satisfaction. The sun was well toward the west, and Ferry could feel weariness crawling through his body in spite of the tension that gripped him. He hadn't slept much last night, and today had offered no opportunity for rest.

Back in the house, with Slim posted in the doorway watching the road to town, Ferry slumped in a chair.

"Maybe we're excited over nothing. Wong Ling could have been mistaken."

"Maybe," Slim agreed. "But I doubt it. If Judd can get Belcher and some of those deputies he had Saturday to ride with him, he'll be here, all right."

Ferry had just started to relax when a volley of shots echoed from down the valley toward town. Lige and Conklin dived for the door, Ferry one step behind them.

To the east of the corral, a wagon was reeling toward the house, the driver hunched over the seat. Seven horsemen thundered along a hundred and fifty yards behind, firing at the careening wagon.

There was no mistaking the giant form of Judd Leighton leading the riders. Just a little behind him was Sheriff Sid Belcher, triggering his gun with the same deadly enthusiasm as his leader. Ferry guessed that the other five riders were men who had served as deputies in the fiasco last Saturday in town. Hired gunmen, nothing more, being paid to finish this war in Leighton's favor.

"Who's in the wagon?" Ferry asked.

"Hugh Bradford," Slim said. "I told you he wouldn't miss a fight."

"That's no fight," Ferry said. "That's murder."

"He's hit!" Corky yelled.

The men surged forward off the veranda as Bradford jerked himself erect, clutching his side.

"He'll never make it," Lige predicted grimly. He fired a shot in the direction of the riders, but the spent bullet kicked up dust just short of its target.

The shot had its effect, however. All the riders except Judd reined up sharply. When Judd saw that he was alone, he jerked his horse around, screaming angrily at the men. They came on then, again firing at the wagon.

Bradford tumbled off the wagon seat and lay just behind the dash, his fingers still locked around the reins. As the wagon thundered past the corral, Ferry turned to Slim.

"Give me cover. I'm going to bring him in."

Before anyone could object, Ferry dashed out to meet the wagon. The tired, frightened team merely swerved enough to miss Ferry, then raced on. Ferry made a dive for the tailgate as the wagon swept past him. Bullets kicked up dust around his feet and tore splinters from the wagon as he clutched the end gate and jerked himself over the edge of the box. He fell flat on the floor, but was up immediately and began crawling toward the front of the wagon.

Ducking under the spring seat, he took the reins from Bradford's slackening grip. He raised his head above the edge of the box to get his bearings, then pulled on the reins. The frightened horse, now nearly spent, yielded slowly.

He guided them around the corner of the house, where he was cut off from the shower of bullets. Sawing on the reins, he brought the horses down to a choppy gallop, then to a nervous trot. He wheeled them into the narrow alley between the house and the bunkhouse and, leaning back hard on the reins, brought them to a halt between the doors opening into the alley from the two buildings.

Some angry curses were shouted from the corral, and those were followed by a new outburst of firing. Evidently Judd had led Belcher's men to believe they would catch the Triangle F unprepared to defend itself.

Ferry quieted the team as quickly as he could. He could hear guns barking on either side of him. Apparently Slim and Corky were shooting from the bunkhouse, while Lige was firing from the house.

When the horses were quiet, Ferry climbed out on the hub of the front wheel. Reaching back over the edge of the box, he lifted Bradford in his arms and stepped down, carrying him into the house. The rancher was still alive, but he had lost consciousness, and Ferry couldn't tell how seriously he was hurt.

Lige came over as Ferry laid him on a couch along the wall. "I know a little about gunshot wounds," he said. "I'll check him over. You take my place at the window."

Ferry hurried to the window, his .45 in his hand. He looked over the deserted yard for a target. A puff of white smoke rose from the corner of the corral, and he fired at it. Another gun belched smoke from the corner of the barn. Two others barked close together from behind the saddle shed.

"See anybody you knew in that bunch except Judd Leighton and Belcher?" Ferry asked Lige.

"Nope," Lige said from the couch where he was still examining Bradford's wounds. "They're all Belcher's hired guns, I reckon. I figure if we can get Belcher and Judd, we'll put an end to the fighting in a hurry."

Ferry turned back, his eyes scanning the yard. Suddenly Lige came over and nudged him.

"Take a look out there on that knoll," he said.

Ferry swept the outer arc beyond the barn and corral with his eyes. "Where?"

"Just to the right of the trail. Looks like Judd and Belcher. Planning some trick, I'll wager. They figure they're beyond the range of a rifle."

"Aren't they?"

"According to how good a shot you are. A bullet will carry that far. But not many men could hit anything at that distance."

Ferry saw the two men then, sitting on their horses, apparently in deep conversation. "You're suggesting that I try?"

"You proved you're the best shot that's hit this country for a long time when you won that horse from Steve. Here's the best rifle on the ranch. Give it a try." He handed a new rifle to Ferry.

Ferry took it reluctantly. "I think they're out of range."

"They think so, too," Lige said. "But they're not out of range of that new rifle you're holding."

Grimly Ferry eased the rifle across the window sill. Judd offered the larger target, but somehow Ferry couldn't bring his sights to bear on that big frame. Accusing black eyes rose up to dim his sight whenever he tried. Rosanne had defied Judd that morning. Maybe she even hated him. But he was her brother. Ferry had seen two of her brothers killed, had wounded another himself. He couldn't be the one to cut down the last of her four brothers unless there was no other way.

The rifle veered over until the squat figure of the sheriff was in the sights. With the sights elevated to compensate for the distance, he squeezed the trigger gently. A second later Belcher rose slightly in the saddle and slid slowly to the ground on the other side of his horse. Judd seemed to freeze for one surprised moment; then he dug in his spurs and bolted for the safety of a neighboring knoll.

"I guess that cut that confab short," Lige said with satisfaction. "That was mighty fine shooting."

Ferry let the rifle slide back off the window sill, feeling sick inside. A groan from the couch took Ferry's mind off Belcher. He turned toward the wounded man in the room.

"He's got to have a doc," Lige said.

"How long before dark?"

"Less than an hour, I reckon," Lige said. "And from the looks of that cloud rolling up in the west, it's going to be plenty dark, too."

"When it's dark, we'll put him back in his wagon and I'll make a run for it."

"That would be suicide," Lige exclaimed. "Let's hope it rains. Maybe Judd's outfit will give up and go home if it does."

An hour dragged by. Shots were exchanged continuously, but so far as Ferry could tell, no damage was done on either side. Black clouds boiled up over the peaks to the west. As darkness settled down, streaks of lightning cut the inky skyline, and the low rumbling echoed from the distant summits.

"Time to try it," Ferry said. "Take out some quilts and put them in the bed of the wagon. I'll bring out Bradford."

"You're crazy," Lige said. But he went into the other room and came back with an armful of blankets.

The team was still standing docilely in the alley between the buildings, apparently glad of the chance to rest after their grueling run.

Slim met Ferry and Lige at the wagon. "What's going on?"

"Bradford's hurt pretty bad," Ferry said. "I'm taking him to the doc."

"You'll never get through that bunch out there."

"I've got to try. How are you and Corky making out?"

"Fine, thanks to those sandbags. Say, who picked off Belcher?"

"I did," Ferry said.

"You didn't kill him," Slim said. "I saw him crawling off down the slope just a while before dark. But figure he's had enough of this fight."

Ferry made Bradford as comfortable as possible in the bed of the wagon, then climbed in and took the reins. He ignored the seat balanced above the level of the box.

"Good luck, Dan," Slim said. "We'll give you cover."

Ferry waited as Slim went back into the bunkhouse and Lige returned to the window in the house. When the guns on either side of him began beating a tattoo in the night, Ferry rose up and slapped the reins. With a yell, he sent the horses leaping away from the protection of the buildings.

XV

For a full half-minute after Ferry lashed the horses into a run across the yard toward the road to town, there was a complete lull in the firing from the corrals. Then the bullets began slapping into the sides of the wagon, sending splinters flying at all angles.

Ferry half expected the men around the corrals to turn their guns on the running horses to bring the wagon to a halt. But they didn't, and the wagon careened out of the yard with neither the horses nor Ferry being hit.

"Are you all right, Bradford?" Ferry asked as the guns died away behind.

"Sure," Bradford said weakly. "But they'll be after us."

Ferry didn't answer. He knew Bradford was right.

Lightning streaked the sky and thunder rolled heavily across the valley as Ferry pushed the horses hard. He reached back and tucked the slicker more securely over Bradford. When the rain started or when the Leightons came after him, he wouldn't have time to tend to the wounded man.

Ferry kept a close watch behind him as each flash of lightning illuminated the road back to the ranch. Three minutes after he broke out of the yard, he saw the horses coming. He could make out only two. But the flashes of lightning didn't give him time to be sure. It told him only that trouble was coming and coming fast.

"They're coming, aren't they?" Bradford asked weakly.

"They're coming," Ferry said.

The next streak of lightning revealed that the riders were nearer and closing the gap rapidly. The team Ferry was driving had had a hard run bringing Bradford to the Triangle F. It had neither the speed nor the endurance to survive another long chase.

The rain struck just as the road swung slightly to the left, cutting through the edge of the timber that stretched down from the ridge. It was there that Ferry and Slim had abandoned their horses the night they had led the Leightons out from Sundown. Ferry realized that his only chance now was to give his pursuers the slip right there. The horses would not keep him ahead of his pursuers for another half-mile.

Lightning ripped the inky sky and thunder hammered across the valley. Rain was coming down in waves until it seemed to Ferry that everything in the storm's path must drown. Glancing back, he couldn't see the last bend in the road even by the brightest flashes of lightning.

To his left an alley between the trees suddenly opened up, leading off toward the ridge, and he wheeled the team into it. Twenty yards from the road, he tooled the wagon in among a sparse stand of pine trees and reined the weary horses to a halt.

Quickly he turned and pulled the slicker tighter around Bradford, pushing the seat of the wagon back until it protected the wounded man's head. Then he dismounted from the wagon and moved around to the front of the team.

Between claps of thunder he heard the running horses on the road and stepped close to his team to keep the animals from making a sound that would give away their presence. But the horses were too tired to care what was running past them. Through the trees, Ferry caught glimpses of the riders by lightning flashes. They were riding with heads down against the pouring rain. Ferry saw only two, and they rode past the tracks he had made in turning off the road without seeing them.

Ferry waited as the rain slackened and finally stopped. If all the men who had descended on the Triangle F that afternoon had taken up the chase, he would have expected them to go on to town and stay there. But there had been only two. They would have to go back to report their failure to catch Ferry.

It was nearly half an hour, Ferry estimated, before the two disgruntled riders splashed back along the road. Whatever tracks the wagon had made in turning off the road must have been wiped out by the rain, for the riders went on without looking to right or left.

Ferry, worried over the long delay and the effect it would have on Bradford, guided the team back to the road and put them to a brisk trot through the mud toward town.

Ferry had little trouble rousing Dr. Robson, who lived in the back of his office. The little bald-headed man with the beady black eyes nodded as Ferry explained his mission.

"Bring him in," he said. "I've been expecting company like this ever since I saw Judd lead that bunch of gunmen out on the Triangle F road."

An hour later, the doctor gave Ferry a report on Bradford. He had been able to stop the bleeding and the wound was not a serious one.

"Can he ride the stage tomorrow?" Ferry asked.

The doctor scratched his head. "I reckon he could if necessary."

"I figure it is. He needs to be some place where he can rest up without holding a gun in his hand, don't you think? He can't do that around Sundown."

The doctor nodded. "I see what you mean. I'll bandage him well in the morning. I figure he can ride as far as Eagle Rock without trouble."

"Good," Ferry said. "That will be far enough. When he's well again he can come back. This will be over one way or another by then."

Ferry checked into the hotel.

In spite of the fact that Ferry had slept but little the night before up in Secret Valley, he barely closed his eyes in his hotel bed. If the attack on the Triangle

F fizzled out and the gunmen came back to town, they night look in the hotel for him.

Toward morning he dropped off to sleep and awoke late. He hurried across the street to the doctor's office. Bradford was much better and was willing to go to Eagle Rock as Ferry had planned. From the doctor's office, Ferry moved down to the restaurant for his breakfast. While he was eating, Connie gave him some news that puzzled him.

"Your lawyer, Sperrel, is in town again."

"What's he doing here?" Ferry asked.

Connie shrugged. "I didn't ask. I thought you'd like to know."

Ferry nodded, paid his bill and went back across the street.

As he stepped up on the veranda of the hotel, Sperrel came out the door. He stopped at the sight of Ferry.

"I thought you were in Ohio," Ferry said.

"Business called me back to this country before I got home," Sperrel explained. "When I got close to Sundown, I just had to stop by and see how you were making out with the Triangle F."

Ferry shook his head. "There's been nothing but

fighting since I came here," he said.

"You haven't found the mine?"

"Haven't had time to make a real search. I have been up to Secret Valley a couple of times, but I didn't see anything there to make a man rich."

"Ad said it was in that valley," the lawyer said thoughtfully. "Don't suppose he was lying, do you?"

Ferry shrugged. "Nobody could predict what Ad would do. But if that mine is in Secret Valley, it must be some freak deposit. There's only a trace of color in the creek. I didn't find anything else. Looks to me like that valley was once a big lake. Maybe there were currents along the bottom that washed all the rocks and sediment, including gold, into a pocket somewhere."

The lawyer nodded. "You could be right, at that. As soon as this fighting allows it, I suppose you'll be searching again. I wish you luck. I'm taking the stage out today."

Ferry went on into the hotel lobby to wait for the stage. Once Bradford was on his way to Eagle Rock, Ferry would ride out to the Triangle F and find out what had happened there.

But before the stage rolled in, seven riders came in

from the direction of the Triangle F. Ferry's nerves tensed as he watched. Two of the riders were wounded, one of them being held in his saddle.

Ferry watched as Judd Leighton pulled up at the Silver Spur. Two of the other men reined in there, too. The two wounded and two of their companions came on, reining up in front of Dr. Robson's office.

The most seriously wounded man was the sheriff, Sid Belcher. The other apparently was one of the hired gunmen who had ridden with the sheriff. Ferry wondered if they would find Bradford in the back of the doctor's office and what they would do if they did find him. But Bradford knew enough to keep out of sight.

A short time after the four men had gone into the doctor's office, the two healthy ones came out. One crossed to the sheriff's office while the other came across to the hotel. Ferry waited for him in the lobby, not at all sure what might happen.

As the man stepped up on the veranda, Ferry eased his gun into his hand while the clerk waved frantically to him.

"Not in here, Mr. Ferry! Please!"

Ferry ignored him and waited. The man came on in and was halfway across the lobby before he saw

Ferry. He halted, his face turning pale.

"Now hold on," he said, raising his hand. "We're out of this thing."

"Since when?" Ferry asked. "And who are 'we'?"

"Belcher hired us but he wasn't putting up the money," the man said hastily as if the speed of his words would convince Ferry of his sincerity. "We're not above fighting for pay. But when Judd Leighton told us we wouldn't get paid unless we finished our job, we quit."

"Who are 'we'?" Ferry pressed, not lowering his gun.

"All the fellows Belcher hired."

"Just Belcher and Judd left?"

"Belcher won't be fighting any more in this scrap," the man said. "Somebody winged him good while he was out there so far he thought sure he was safe."

"You're pulling out?" Ferry asked.

"Soon as we get our gear together. Most of it is here in the hotel."

Ferry hesitated. "What's Judd going to do?"

"Ask him," the man said. "Any objection to my getting my gear and clearing out?"

Ferry lowered the gun. "I reckon not. But be sure

you get a long way from here. I don't ever want to see you again."

"It's not likely you will," the man said, and hurried toward the stairs leading up to the second floor rooms.

Ferry, keeping an eye on the saloon down the street, crossed to the doctor's office. As he reached it, the wounded man who had been one of Belcher's deputies came out. He barely looked at Ferry as he hurried across to the hotel, his arm in a tight sling.

Ferry found Belcher lying on the couch in the doctor's outer office. The deputy had been right; Belcher wouldn't be fighting any more in this war. But he didn't look as if he were seriously wounded.

From the doctor's office Ferry looked for the stage. He saw the five deputies ride out of town but he didn't see Judd leave. If Judd stayed in town, Ferry expected trouble when he tried to get Bradford on the stage.

The stage rolled in then. But before Ferry called Bradford out, he stepped out on the porch where he could see the hitchrack in front of the Silver Spur. Judd's horse was gone. Dan's eyes swept the street. It wasn't like Judd to sneak out of town. Yet if he hid ridden down the street on his way home, Ferry would surely have seen him.

Every muscle and nerve was alert as Ferry led Hugh Bradford up the street to the stage office. Ferry found some consolation in the fact that the stage office was at the far end of town from the saloon. If Judd Leighton was still in the saloon, he was a long way from the stage station.

There was no unusual stir in town as Bradford got on the stage and the coach rolled down the street on its way to Eagle Rock, eighteen miles away.

It was only after the coach had disappeared that Ferry remembered that Sperrel had said he was going to leave Sundown today on the stage. What could have caused him to change his mind? Ferry frowned as he thought about it. Why had Sperrel come back to Sundown in the first place? And why hadn't he taken the stage out that morning as he'd said he was going to?

But before Ferry had time to find a reasonable answer, he saw three riders come into the south end of town, and all thoughts of the lawyer left his mind.

He hurried down the street to meet the riders, noting the tenseness with which they rode, their eyes darting up and down the street, pausing to examine every horse at each hitchrack. They paused momentarily at the Silver Saloon; then, seeing Ferry coming toward them, they rode on to the hotel to meet him.

"Everything quiet on the ranch, Slim?" Ferry asked.

"Too quiet," Slim said, his eyes still searching the town. "Where are those so-called gun fighters who are so anxious to shoot as long as nobody shoots back?"

"If you mean Belcher's deputies, they rode out of town a few minutes ago."

"Quit the fight?" Lige Conklin asked.

Ferry nodded. "They'd had enough. Judd refused to pay them because they didn't finish their job."

"How about Belcher?" Slim asked.

"He's in the doc's office. He won't be fighting any more for a while."

"Where's Judd?"

"I don't know," Ferry said. "He was in the Silver Spur the last I knew. But his horse isn't there any more."

"He's not there now," Corky Wills said. "If he had been, he'd have plugged one or two of us as we went past. What now, Slim?"

"I'm going to talk to Belcher. If his hired gun hands have quit, then all we've got to do is gun down Judd and the thing is over."

Slim strode across the street, with Corky and Lige at his heels. Ferry hesitated a moment, then tagged along, too.

XVI

Ferry stood on the porch of the hotel and watched Slim and Lige and Corky ride down the street and disappear around the bend on the trail out to the Triangle F. Then he turned to go into the hotel. If Sperrel was still there, he intended to find out why.

But he stopped when Ed Hartlett called to him from his grocery store across the street. Ferry frowned. He had little use for the grocer, who sided with the Leightons. Nevertheless, he crossed the street, his caution increasing with every step.

On the porch of the store, he stopped. "What do you want, Hartlett?"

"I've got a message for you, Ferry."

"Who from? Judd?"

Hartlett shook his head. "From Rosanne. She wants

you to meet her by the big rock on Thunder Ridge."

Ferry studied the storekeeper's face suspiciously.

"When did she tell you that?"

"Just a few minutes ago."

"I was right here in town. Why didn't she tell me herself?"

"Because Judd was here in town, too. And she didn't want him to see her."

Ferry rubbed his chin, unable to get rid of the suspicion that sent prickles up and down his spine. The storekeeper was a weak character, one Ferry couldn't trust. But it was possible that Rosanne did want to see him.

"I'll think it over," he said, and turned off the porch.

"She said she was going there from here and would be waiting for you," Hartlett said to Ferry's back.

Ferry went down the street to the livery stable and rented a horse. He didn't trust Hartlett, but he knew he would ride back to the Triangle F by way of Thunder Ridge and the big rock. If Rosanne was there as Hartlett had said she would be, it might be something good could come of it.

He rode slowly down the street to Kitter's store and

turned into the side street there. The street ran out into a trail that passed Bradford's ranch and climbed the end of the ridge. He had ridden that trail the first day he had been in the country. Although it had been only a few days ago, it seemed like months.

He passed along the side of Kitter's Hardware. As he reached the rear, a woman stepped out from the back of the store and blocked his way. The horse shied violently, and Ferry had to grab the horn of the saddle to keep from being thrown.

He barely recognized Mamie with her hair hanging in strings over her blood-smeared face. There were scratches on her arms as she held them up to stop Ferry.

"I've got something to tell you, Ferry," she said through bruised lips.

He nodded. "I'm listening. What happened to you?"

"It was Link Dalton," Mamie said. "I'll settle with him later. Judd told him that I was to be cut in on that mine of yours."

Ferry leaned forward. "You lost me. What does Judd have to say about any mine I own?"

"He figures to get it. And I reckon he will. He offered me a slice of it for helping him set Steve

Hayes up for that knifing. Evidently he made a deal with Dalton, too. I see through him now. Judd plans to get it all for himself. He'll cut Dalton out, too, if he can. He never figured on keeping his bargain with me."

"Is that what you wanted to tell me?" Ferry asked.

"No!" Mamie's voice had the cut of a whiplash. "Judd Leighton will never live to get that mine! I'll see to that!"

"Are you going gunning for him?"

"You're going to do that for me," Mamie said. "Don't think I came out here to pass the time of day with you because I like you, Ferry. I aim to help you kill Judd Leighton."

"I wasn't starting out to kill Judd right now," Ferry said.

"Oh, yes, you are," Mamie said, her eyes shining feverishly. "You're heading out to meet Rosanne on the ridge, aren't you?"

Ferry frowned. "How did you know that?"

"It's a trap, Ferry. Judd will be waiting to ambush you. If you know it, I figure you can beat him to it." Her pale blue eyes bored into Ferry. "I don't care what happens to you, Ferry. I just want you to live long enough to kill Judd Leighton!"

She turned back down the alley, and Ferry watched her go.

With a heavy sigh, he nudged his horse into motion.

He rode cautiously along the ridge, barely aware of the peaceful quiet that surrounded him. Every tree and rock that could conceal a man drew his full attention. But nothing stirred, and Ferry began to doubt Mamie's story.

Then the winding trail straightened out, and a hundred yards ahead he could see the big rock. Rosanne was sitting at the base of the small pine that grew on the sunny side of the rock.

So it had been Hartlett who had told the truth; not Mamie. He nudged his horse forward. But as he advanced, a prickly sensation ran up his spine. Although Rosanne was facing him, she made no move to indicate that she even saw him. That wasn't right.

He eased the horse to a slower pace. Still Rosanne didn't move. The suspicion crowding into his mind was suddenly confirmed as Rosanne screamed. A bullet kicked up dust in front of Ferry's horse, and he left the saddle in a long dive. He rolled behind a big pine close to the trail, his gun coming into his hand.

The picture was clear now. Mamie had told the truth. Judd had laid an ambush, and he had used Rosanne as bait. It had almost worked, too. Evidently Judd had been so sure that Ferry would ride closer that he hadn't been ready to shoot when Rosanne screamed. If Judd had been ready, Ferry would have been dead now.

Leaving the protection of the big pine, he glided forward. Judd's shot had come from behind the big rock. Ferry couldn't risk shooting that way for fear of hitting Rosanne.

As he came closer to the rock, Ferry's caution increased. Then he caught a glimpse of Judd moving down among the boulders that bordered the steep trail on the Triangle F side of the ridge. The huge rocks rested precariously on the slope that, just a few yards down, broke off into a hundred foot sheer cliff.

Those rocks offered Judd perfect protection and put Ferry at a disadvantage as he dodged among the trees on the ridge. Judd opened fire again, but none of his shots found their mark. Ferry answered each one with a shot of his own, although he knew that his chances of scoring a hit depended entirely on luck.

Then Ferry, trying to get into a better position to

press the battle, passed close to the big rock. Rosanne was still sitting by the little tree. Anger burned through Ferry as he saw that her hands were tied behind the tree. He wheeled toward her, but a close shot from Judd emphasized the folly of trying to free Rosanne while Judd had a gun.

He emptied his gun at the rock hiding Judd, anger overpowering his reason. He ran his hand along his belt for more bullets and stopped in sudden consternation. The belt was empty.

He'd have to go back to his horse for more shells. Then he remembered that he was riding a rented horse from the livery stable in Sundown. There would be no ammunition there, either. He could either beat a cautious retreat or try to find some way to even the odds against him.

He was in the edge of the boulder field now, and his eye fell on the rubble at his feet. Stopping, he selected some small rocks and threw one a little to his left. Judd scooted around his rock to keep it between him and the sound, firing at the rocks where the little stone had fallen.

Cautiously Ferry repeated his act, throwing each rock a little farther to his left. Judd shifted and fired each time a rock fell. Evidently Judd had lost track of Ferry after his final burst of shots and was sure he was now moving where those rocks were falling. Ferry couldn't help thinking how easy it would have been to end the fight if he had only had some ammunition for his gun, because Judd had moved around in plain sight of him.

Silently Ferry stole closer to Judd, dodging from one boulder to another. Judd was scanning the rocks in the opposite direction, convinced now that Ferry was over there. At intervals, Ferry would throw one of his small rocks over Judd's head, letting it fall a little closer to Jud each time.

The rocks brought an occasional shot from Judd, and as they began getting closer to him, he retreated from one rock to another. Ferry knew that the deception wouldn't last much longer. Judd was exposing himself more and more to get a glimpse of what he was shooting at. Any moment now, he would discover the trick.

Ferry's advance and Judd's retreat had brought them within ten yards of each other. Ferry knew that now was his one and only chance to equal the odds. Moving as silently as a shadow, he left the protection of his rock and crept toward Judd.

Then, within five feet of Judd's back, Ferry moved a tiny rock with his foot, and Judd wheeled. His eyes seemed about to pop from their sockets. Then he jerked up his gun as Ferry sprang forward.

Ferry struck the gun just as it exploded, the bullet smashing into a rock and ricocheting into space with a shrill whine. The gun was jolted from Judd's grasp and scooted across the rocks to drop into a crevice.

With a bellow, Judd surged against Ferry. But Ferry was already dodging away, landing stinging blows as he retreated. Judd completely ignored the blows, charging at Ferry, murder in his eyes.

Ferry realized he dare not let Judd get him in his grasp. And those blows he was landing seemed only to irritate Judd as the bullets from a toy rifle might irritate a bear.

Then Ferry stumbled as he dodged one of Judd's charges. He went down, and Judd roared with triumph as he turned to pin him. Ferry twisted away, then gasped as he found himself looking over the edge of the sheer drop that ended over a hundred feet below in a jungle of jagged rocks.

With a burst of strength, Ferry surged to his feet and

retreated up the slope. He was tiring rapidly. He knew he wouldn't be able to keep away from Judd indefinitely.

Judd came up the slope after him, and suddenly Ferry knew what he had to try. Maybe he could do it and maybe he couldn't. But now was his only chance.

He suddenly drove forward to meet Judd's charge. Judd's eyes bulged in surprise and he almost dropped his guard. Ferry drove his fists into Judd's stomach with all the strength he had.

With a grunt, Judd gave ground. He dropped his guard, and Ferry switched his attack to his face. Judd backed off again, trying to regain his composure and his balance. But Ferry gave him no chance. With all his remaining strength, he pounded Judd backward.

Then suddenly Judd lurched up straight, trying mightily to halt his backward movement. One foot had stepped out into space, only the toe catching the edge of the cliff.

For one long ageless moment he teetered on the brink, his arms flaying the air like the wings of a wounded eagle. His eyes bulged from his face. Slowly he began to lose the battle to regain his balance. Then with a horror-filled scream that echoed from the rocks long the ridge, he lurched out into space and disppeared.

Ferry leaned against a rock, fighting to regain his reath, a wave of sickness washing over him. Then he lade his way slowly back up the slope to the big ock, fumbling in his pocket for his knife to cut the opes holding Rosanne. His weary fingers would never e able to untie the knots.

When the ropes were cut, Rosanne stood up. But 'erry didn't look at her. After all, Judd had been her rother. He didn't know what to expect from her, and t the moment he was too weary to care much.

He was barely aware that she had turned to the tree nd kneeled beside it, her fingers probing under the ock behind the tree. A moment later she stood up .gain, something in her hand.

"Look what I found, Dan." She held out an en-'elope with writing scrawled over it.

"What is it?" he asked, his mind still a little fuzzy.

"It's a letter," she said. "I felt it with my fingers in hat crack under the big rock while I was tied to the .ree. It's yours, Dan."

He took the letter and tried to hold it steady, but his muscles refused to obey. He did make out the name in the corner. Addison Ferry. He handed it back to Rosanne. "I guess I'll have to ask you to read it to me."

"I will if you want me to," she said quietly.

Ferry sank wearily against the rock. "Why did Ad leave it here?"

"This writing on the outside explains that," Rosanne said. " 'I know I'll never get to mail this, Dan. Judd is out there in the rocks with a rifle. He'll get me soon. I hope you find this.' "

Rosanne stopped, and Ferry nodded. "What's on the inside?"

She tore open the envelope. There were several pages written in a big crude scrawl. Rosanne smoothed the pages in her lap.

" 'Dear Dan,' " she began: " 'I want you to come to the Triangle F as soon as you can. You'll walk into a fight, but you'll inherit this ranch as soon as I die. You'll get all that I have, including the mine.

" 'I've been confiding in my lawyer, Sperrel, but lately I've become suspicious of him. I think he'd like to have that mine, too. I've told Sperrel how to get to Secret Valley, but I haven't told him how to find the mine itself. I hope you get here in time for me to show you, but I doubt if you will. Secret Valley is straight up the valley behind the ranch. If Sperrel is on the level, he'll tell you how to get there.' "

Rosanne stopped reading and looked at Ferry. "Did the lawyer tell you or did you find it yourself?"

"He told me," Ferry said. "More than likely Ad was getting suspicious of everyone. That's what comes from having something as valuable as a mine."

Rosanne went back to the letter. " 'The gold is in a pocket in Secret Valley. That valley was once a lake with the outlet over the top. All the heavy rocks and sediment dropped into a ravine just below that outlet. It was too heavy to be lifted over the top. There are pounds and pounds of gold in that ravine. When the lake was drained, the gold stayed right there.

" 'After Jig Ailey, my partner, found that deposit, we built a cabin directly over the ravine. The front part is the living room, and behind the burlap sacks on the back wall is a door leading into the mine. We carried the dirt we took out to another ravine and dumped it.

" 'At first we packed the ore out on Jig's burros. Then Jig found a girl lost up toward Secret Valley and was fool enough to take her to his cabin. I got Jig to promise not to show her the mine, and I think he kept that promise.

" 'After she came, Jig and I dug the ore loose in the daytime, one of us watching to see that the girl didn't get too close. Then at night we took it outside while the girl was asleep. We pounded it into dust by the stream and washed out the gold.

" 'After Jig was killed, the girl left. I kept pounding the ore and washing out the gold. I was sure I was being watched when I came down to the ranch. One day Matt Lundo trailed me into the valley and we had a running fight. I killed him, and Judd Leighton threatened to kill me. I reckon he will some day.

" 'When trouble started, all my regular hands quit except one, a fellow named Link Dalton. I fired him because I didn't trust him. I hired a crew of gunmen to protect me. Watch out for Dalton.' "

"So that's where Dalton fits in," Ferry said. "Does Ad say any more about him?"

"There's not much more in the letter," Rosanne said, and smoothed the pages in her lap. " 'There is a little box of gold dust just inside the mine door. I've washed that out since Jig was killed. I've been afraid to bring it out. Get it first thing. Just don't let Judd Leighton or Link Dalton get it.

" 'I'm going to try to fool Judd tonight. He watches the valley road to town all the time, so I'm going to take the ridge road. He won't expect me there. Come as soon as you can, Dan. If I'm dead when you get here, carry on the fight. Good luck. Addison Ferry.' "

Rosanne laid down the letter. Ferry sighed. "That sounds just like Ad. Wants me to be sure to get that little box of gold dust. He would rather let his enemies have the whole mine than that box of dust he cleaned himself."

Rosanne suddenly jerked away from the rock. "I just remembered. Link Dalton rode up here from Sundown with Judd. They argued about the bargain they made. Link thought Judd was double-crossing him. Judd wanted Link to help spring this ambush on you. But after Judd tied me to this tree, Dalton rode on to Secret Valley to look for that mine. Judd was going to meet him there after he sprang the trap on you."

Ferry pushed to his feet. "I'll have to go after him. He can't help finding the mine now that the cabin is gone."

Rosanne got to her feet, too. "I'm going with you."

"Even after what happened?"

Her face lost some of its color, but her black eyes

were ablaze with life. "After what Judd has done lately, he didn't even seem like a brother. Anyway, there are other things stronger than family ties."

She said no more, but turned and walked to her horse, which was tied in the trees beyond the big rock. Ferry watched her go before starting to look for his horse.

XVII

The sun had vanished behind the high ridge when Dan Ferry and Rosanne reached the base of the wall blocking entrance to Secret Valley. By the time they had climbed the trough to the top, darkness had settled over everything, and Ferry called a halt until the moon, already lighting the east with a yellowish glow, got high enough to light their way.

"He must be in the valley now," Ferry said. "He can't get out past us, so we'll wait till we can see what we're doing."

"He may have a trap set," Rosanne said. "He's expecting Judd to come, you know. He'll kill us as quick as he would Judd. If he found the mine, he'd try to kill Judd so he'd have it all himself. You're the only one standing between him and the mine now."

Ferry nodded. "An ambush would be just his caliber."

When the moon had risen high enough to light the trough across the top of the wall and cast deep shadows into the valley beyond, Ferry mounted again. With Rosanne a few yards behind him, Ferry picked his way cautiously through the rocky trench until he reached the point where it broke out into the trail leading down to the bottom of Secret Valley.

"You'd better stay here till I find out what's down there," Ferry suggested.

"I've come this far; I'm not going to stop here," Rosanne said. "Do you have your gun loaded?"

Ferry remembered then. "I haven't got a shell to my name," he said, frustration overcoming him.

She laughed softly. "You see, you need me along." She reached back into her saddle bag. "I brought along an extra box Judd had. Load up."

Gratefully he took the ammunition. He loaded his gun and stuffed extra shells into his gun belt. Then he nudged his horse down the trail.

With every nerve as taut as a steel wire, Ferry let his horse pick his way down the steep trail. The valley was quiet; too quiet. Ferry couldn't down the feeling that Dalton was watching every move he made, waiting for the exact moment to strike.

Then, just as the horse reached the level of the valley floor, a bullet slapped the air past Ferry's ear. His reaction was instantaneous as he dived off his horse into the trees flanking the trail.

Another bullet thudded into a tree trunk only inches from his head. Ferry hugged the ground, exposing himself only enough to get a line on the location of the gunman.

He was to the left of the trail, close to the pool where the river was sucked into the crevice that tunneled under the wall. Some trees and a maze of boulders made a veritable fortress of the area between the trail and the pool.

Ferry scrambled over behind a boulder where he was safe for the moment from the probing shots of the gunman. He fired twice at the flash of the bushwhacker's gun but knew he was just wasting his ammunition.

He looked back up the trail at Rosanne. She had dismounted, but she wasn't staying with her horse. He tried to motion her back, but she came running down the trail, ducking into the trees as soon as she reached them. A minute later she dropped on her knees beside

Ferry.

"Are you hurt, Dan?"

"Not a scratch," Ferry said. "But it wasn't my fault. I certainly wasn't expecting him here. I thought he might be in those thick trees just ahead. The light must have been bad or he wouldn't have missed."

"He's down in those rocks by the pool. You'll never flush him out from here."

Ferry nodded. "You've got that figured. I may have to wait him out."

"That's what he'll expect," Rosanne said. She held out her .38. "Let's trade guns. You circle around to his left and get the drop on him. I'll keep him busy with your gun. He'll never suspect that you're not right here."

Ferry shook his head. "He might get lucky shooting at you."

"I've been shot at before; I know enough to keep my head down. If we wait long enough, he might pick us both off."

Ferry couldn't argue with that logic. Handing her his gun, he took her .38 and began a cautious circle to come up on the gunman from the other side. Behind him, Rosanne fired and got an immediate answer.

Ferry moved hurriedly but with extreme caution. As long as the gunman didn't suspect what he was doing, he wasn't in much danger of being spotted. The low roar of the falls above muffled all sounds but the sharp bark of the six-guns.

Swinging wide, Ferry reached the river a hundred yards above the hidden gunman. Boulders were scattered all along the bank, half buried in the ground and the lush grass. Slowly he began his advance, dodging from one boulder to another.

Then he picked up his pace as he realized that Rosanne was no longer firing. At first the terrifying thought struck him that she had been hit. Then he realized that she was probably out of ammunition. Her gun belt would have .38 ammunition in it. She had given him all the shells for the .45, and he had left the box in his saddle bag.

The moon had swung high enough to reach the pool, making it look inky black where it whirled into the crevice at the base of the wall. Ferry picked out the rock hiding the gunman; then, as the man shifted slightly, Ferry saw him clearly. He was still facing Rosanne's gun, but apparently he was becoming suspicious of the lull in the shooting.

Ferry glided forward, hoping to get much closer before being detected. But luck was against him. Some noise or movement caught the attention of the gunman, and he whirled to face Ferry. Ferry was in the open between two boulders. The man's hasty shot snapped past Dan and ricocheted off the top of a boulder behind him.

Ferry dug in his heels, bringing up the .38 and firing almost in one motion. The gunman lurched back against the rock, his gun dropping from his hand. His left hand came across to grasp his right shoulder.

Ferry dashed forward. "Don't do it, Dalton," he shouted as the man started to lunge toward his gun.

The man straightened, a bitter laugh coming from him. "You've got the wrong man, Dan."

Ferry stopped short as he realized this man was not Link Dalton. He was short but not nearly as heavy.

"Sperrel!"

As Ferry fought to control his surprise, the lawyer made another stab for his gun with his good hand. Ferry checked it with a sharp order.

"Keep away from that gun!"

Sperrel backed against the rock like a cornered wild-cat. Then he seemed to relax, a thin smile parting his ips. "Now that you've caught me, what are you going to do with me?"

"Take you in to stand trial, I guess," Ferry said.

"On what charges?"

"You're a lawyer; you ought to know. Trying to steal a mine that belonged to your client might be a starter."

The lawyer shook his head. "You won't take me in to stand trial, Dan. Remember, I'm wounded."

"A .38 slug in the shoulder won't keep you from facing a jury."

"I wouldn't bet on that."

Ferry frowned, trying to understand the significance of the lawyer's words. Rosanne appeared then, running toward them through the scattered boulders. She stopped beside Ferry.

"Mr. Sperrel!" she gasped. "Where's Link Dalton?"

"Over there, buried under some rocks," Sperrel said carelessly, pointing upstream.

"Buried?" Ferry echoed. "Did you kill him?"

"He was double-crossing me," the lawyer said.

"What dealing did you have with Dalton?"

"He was my nephew."

A light suddenly dawned on Ferry. "You were trying to get old Ad's mine all the time. You planted Dalton on the Triangle F to find out where the mine was."

"You're catching on," Sperrel said easily as if he wanted to talk. Ferry didn't discourage him. "Ad wouldn't tell me exactly where the mine was, so I hired Link to get a job on the ranch and find it for me. I should have known he'd mess it up or, if he found it, he'd double-cross me."

"Did Link kill Jig Ailey?" Rosanne asked suddenly.

"Yes," Sperrel said. "The fool! Tortured him, trying to make him tell where the mine was."

"And Judd got the blame for it," Ferry said. "I suppose Dalton tried to get the mine for himself."

Sperrel nodded. "I got proof of it when Link beat up Mamie because Judd had promised her a share of the mine. I saw through the whole double-crossing scheme then. I came up here to look for the mine or Link, whichever I could find. I found Link."

"And killed him," Rosanne finished.

"What else?" Sperrel shrugged. "If Ad hadn't gotten suspicious of me, I wouldn't have had to hire

ink." He smiled. "I should have kept you out of it,
o, Dan. I could have let you believe he left the ranch
me. But I thought maybe he'd told you where the
ine was, and it would be easier to let you show me
here it was than to find it myself."

"You never went back to Ohio at all," Ferry ex-
aimed.

"Of course not. I couldn't find the mine there."

"Now you'll have to face several charges," Ferry
aid. "I suppose nobody can prove it wasn't a fair
ght between you and Dalton."

"Nobody will get the chance to try." Sperrel smiled
gain. "I'm wounded, remember?"

Ferry frowned. The lawyer's wound wasn't a serious
ne and he knew it. "That won't keep you out of
ourt."

Rosanne suddenly pointed a finger at the lawyer.
You're afraid of Connie, aren't you?"

"Connie?" Ferry exclaimed. "Why would he be
fraid of her?"

"I don't know," Rosanne admitted. "But I was with
er one day in town when we saw Mr. Sperrel. Connie
aid she'd see him hang some day. Then she shut up
nd wouldn't say another word."

Sperrel leaned back against the boulder behind him his eyes on the inky water of the pool. "She'd like that," he said almost as if talking to himself.

"What's she got to do with you?" Ferry asked.

"She's my niece, Link's cousin. When Link failed to get results, I sent Connie up here. She was to get lost up in the valley and let Jig Ailey find her and take her in. He did. But Connie didn't try to find out anything. She knew I couldn't make her tell something she didn't know."

"That's hardly reason enough to make her want to see you hang."

"I was in business with her father after my sister Connie's mother, died," Sperrel said, showing a surprising willingness to tell the whole story. "We fought one night over a deal, and I killed him. Connie saw it. Connie was thirteen then. I took her in and raised her, threatening to kill her if she ever said a word about what she'd seen. But if I was brought into court she'd jump at the chance to tell all she knows."

"I wouldn't blame her," Ferry said after a moment. "She's waited long enough. She'll soon get her chance. Let's get started back to Sundown."

Sperrel pushed away from the rock. "I told you I'd

never get to court," he said softly. "This is as far as I go."

Ferry, suddenly understanding what the lawyer meant, leaped forward. But he was too late. Sperrel launched himself out into the pool.

For one complete circle, he seemed to float on the wildly whirling water. Then, like a sliver of wood, he was sucked into the vortex of the whirlpool and disappeared. Rosanne turned away with a shudder.

"Looks like he won his last case," Ferry said after a time. "No court will ever convict him of murder now."

It was an hour later when Dan Ferry and Rosanne reached the top of the climb out of Secret Valley. Ferry was leading two horses, Link Dalton's bay and Sperrel's horse, a black with a white belt over its hips.

Ferry stopped and dismounted, letting his horse blow. As he stood looking out over the valley, he marveled at the peaceful scene that covered the tragedy in its depths. The faint murmur of the falls reached his ears. The moon, now well up in the heavens, silvered the valley.

"It's beautiful, isn't it?"

Ferry turned to look at Rosanne at his elbow. "It is till you think that it's been the cause of so much trouble."

"Let's forget that, Dan. It's all in the past."

"Can you forget it all, Rosanne? Judd, the twins?"

She didn't answer immediately, her eyes on the valley below. "Yes, Dan, I think I can forget that this trouble ever stood between us. Nothing we can do will change it now. Today's gone. There'll be to-morrow."

He reached out for her, and she came to him willingly. There would be tomorrow, many tomorrows. And they would be wonderful days.